Revenge in Sweetwater

Landgrabbers in the Wild West didn't always have it their own way, as Albert Bothwell found out when he tried to drive Jim Averell and his lover Ellie Watson from their homesteads. When Jim Averell is killed, Bothwell thinks he has won, except that broken-hearted Ellie Watson decides to take her revenge by carrying the fight right into the heart of his cattle-ranching empire.

By taking on a loan woman Bothwell breaks one of the cowboy codes of behaviour and his right-hand man doesn't like it. His defection to Ellie Watson's side tips the balance in her favour. Even so, Ellie has to fight lead with lead and the outcome is always in doubt.

Revenge in Sweetwater

Derek Taylor

A Black Horse Western

ROBERT HALE · LONDON

© Derek Taylor 2004
First published in Great Britain 2004

ISBN 0 7090 7458 1

Robert Hale Limited
Clerkenwell House
Clerkenwell Green
London EC1R 0HT

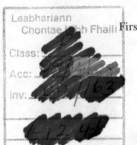
Typeset by
Derek Doyle & Associates, Liverpool.
Printed and bound in Great Britain by
Antony Rowe Limited, Wiltshire

ONE

Jim Averell was sitting on his mount looking out over his one hundred and sixty acres. He loved Wyoming and he loved particularly the spot that he could call home, his, that is. It was on Sweetwater River in Sweetwater County. But more to the point it was adjacent to the homestead of Ellen Watson, the woman he loved. She loved him, too, which meant their lives on Sweetwater River could be happy. Trouble was someone else wanted their land and was not going to give up until they got it.

'But they ain't gonna get it. At least not while I live and breathe,' Averell muttered to himself, pulling his horse's reins to turn and ride home. He lived in a property that doubled as a roadhouse for weary travellers and hungry cowboys. Rumour had it that Ellen Watson, who helped him run the place, served the cowboys in ways other than simply filling their bellies. But this was a vile slur on a decent and hardworking character and Jim Averell had let it be known far and wide that he'd kill anyone who voiced so dirty a lie in his hearing.

It wasn't long before he was dismounting outside his roadhouse. As he tied up his mount to the hitching rail, thinking he'd unsaddle her later, he noticed there were five other horses there. Could be business, he thought, could be trouble. His right hand naturally went to the Colt he had in the holster that hung down on his right hip. It was reassuringly there, with a full barrel. Just in case. Just in case. He knew, though, the moment he stepped into the building that the men sitting at a table near the bar worked for local rancher Albert John Bothwell, a big shot in the local Stock Growers' Association. He knew too that they weren't there just to wash the dirt of the trail out of their craws.

Walking up to the bar where Ellen, or 'Ellie', as he called her, was standing, he threw them a casual glance. The glance they collectively threw back was pregnant with vicious intent. It unnerved him but he didn't let it show.

'All right?' he said to Ellie affectionately, approaching her.

'Fine, love,' she replied, telling him, though, with a tilt of her head that they soon might not be.

She was right.

'Since you weren't here when we arrived, I thought you must have taken Bothwell's advice and gone altogether,' a tough-looking cowpoke named Joe South remarked. He was the one obviously in charge of the group of men sitting at the table.

'I told Bothwell this place ain't for sale and that it ain't ever gonna be. So I ain't going nowhere,' Averell replied tersely, turning to face him.

'We know that,' South replied, 'but it don't mean you ain't leaving.'

Bothwell's ranch was on the Sweetwater River. Ellen Watson's and Jim Averell's homesteads were right in the middle of prime rangeland claimed by Bothwell. Their homesteads gave them the rights over more than a mile of Horse Creek, whose waters emptied into Sweetwater River. This made

7

Bothwell's empire-building difficult and he didn't like it, which meant only one thing for Watson and Averell: trouble, and South and the others were there to bring it to them.

'Look,' Averell said, 'we don't want any trouble here, boys. We're here legally. You're drinking in our establishment and we ain't asking no one for any trouble.'

Joe South and his men looked at one another in amused contempt. They were being paid decent money by Bothwell to show Averell and his ladyfriend that he, Bothwell, meant business; they felt they had been given a licence to kill, if need be. And killing was something they were not squeamish about.

'Well,' South declared, 'that's a pretty statement you just made but it don't tell the whole truth. The Association knows you been rustling their cattle and that's a hanging offence. But that ain't the only way folks like you can die.'

There were other people eating and drinking in the roadhouse but they didn't want any part of the trouble that was brewing around them. Some of them got busier with what they were doing there, others simply looked on to see what was going to happen next. It was Ellen Watson who showed them what that was going to be.

'Best you boys drink up and get outa here,' she informed South and his men, stepping forward to make her point. She wasn't pretty and didn't cut any kind of imposing figure but she looked determined. Averell lifted his left hand to indicate to her that he'd handle the situation.

'You heard what the lady said. Now get outa here before I throw you out,' he said to South.

Standing up and kicking his chair out from behind him, South went for his gun. But before he could do anything effective with it Averell drew his own and shot it out of his hand. Beads of sweat formed instantly on Averell's forehead but he stuck to his ground, letting South's men know he'd kill any one of them who went for his gun.

South's shooting hand would never be any good to him again. It was a bloody mess. It was a warning to the others and none of them tried anything.

'Get him,' South ordered them, wincing with pain.

The expression on Averell's face dared them to try it. The fact that his gun was cocked and ready persuaded them they'd better leave.

'You ain't gonna get away with this,' one of them said.

'We'll be back with a rope for each of you,' another added.

'Tell Bothwell to do his own dirty work next time,' Ellen Watson sneered at him reply.

South said nothing more. His hand was bleeding badly and he was beginning to feel faint. Ineffectually trying to throw a threatening look at Averell and Watson he followed his men out of the roadhouse. He'd have collapsed on the steps outside had not one of his men rushed to help him.

'Maybe now Bothwell will realize he doesn't frighten us,' Ellen Watson said to Averell as he uncocked his gun and returned it to its holster.

'I wouldn't count on it,' was all Averell said in reply, reaching for a bottle of whiskey.

TWO

'Dr Ritchie had to amputate what was left of his hand,' Henry Durbin, one of the gang who had accompanied Joe South to Jim Averell's roadhouse, was informing Albert Bothwell.

A look of consternation spread across Bothwell's face. He wasn't remotely concerned about South's injury but he was worried about the way things were getting out of control.

'Henderson saw Ellen Watson stealing our cattle, ain't that enough?' he barked, making Durbin take a step backwards. 'I sent Joe to tell the whore and her pimp this and to give them one last chance to clear out of Sweetwater. How many of you were there?'

'Six,' Durbin replied sheepishly.

'Six?' Bothwell remarked incredulously. 'And Joe South goes and gets his hand shot off and nobody does anything!'

'Averell drew first,' Durbin said weakly.

Bothwell grunted contemptuously in reply and then he was pensively quiet for a second or two.

'Go hang both of them. Now, and don't come back until you have done so,' he suddenly instructed Durbin firmly.

As Durbin left his office Bothwell's only concern was that he should carry out his orders to the letter. Things like this have to be nipped in the bud, he thought to himself, as he picked up that week's *Casper's Weekly Journal* and scanned what Averell had written in it:

Landgrabbers are only camped here as speculators under the Desert Land Act. They are opposed to anything that would settle and improve the country or make it anything but a cow pasture for Eastern speculators. Is it not enough to excite one's prejudice to see Sweetwater River opened, or claimed, for a distance of seventy-five miles from its mouth, by three or four men?

The article had already been discussed at a meeting of the Stock Growers' Association and a consensus had been taken that Jim Averell was a menace in their midst who was not going to be tolerated. The fact that he had recently been made a justice of the peace only served to reinforce this feeling. What made it worse was that the man was known to run what everyone knew was only a cover for a whorehouse. Sweetwater should be a God-fearing, law-abiding county, was Bothwell's justification for what he had ordered Durbin to do, and throwing down the newspaper on to his desk, he was confident it was all the cover he needed to grab Ellen Watson and Jim Averell's land to get the rights to the water he needed to consolidate his already extensive landholdings in the county.

Averell and Ellie were nervous about leaving one another alone, but Averell had a right-hand man at the roadhouse and he said he had to go into town to get some provisions and that she'd be all right with him. In fact as well as Mick O'Brien there were two other hired hands who helped out with the work around the roadhouse and whose jobs now also included keeping their eyes peeled for any signs of trouble.

'But what about you?' Ellie asked Averell, as he prepared to leave.

'I'll be all right. Josh here will be with me riding shotgun. We'll be more than a match for any trouble that might come our way.'

But Ellie wasn't convinced and was full of apprehension as she watched him and Josh ride away on a buckboard.

'They'll be all right.' Mick O'Brien tried to reassure her. 'Jim's a justice of the peace now and the law won't take kindly to anyone trying to intimidate him.'

'It didn't seem to bother Bothwell none yesterday. Don't see why it should bother him now.'

O'Brien didn't have a reply to this, other than to determine to make sure no harm came to Ellie while Averell was away. Ellie sensed this and was grateful for it. Though she felt that when the chips were down she was more than capable of taking care of herself. She might have been right but it always depended on the odds, as Jim Averell was about to find out.

He hadn't gone five miles east down the old Oregon Trail, when he was confronted by Henry Durbin and his men.

'Do you see what I see?' Josh remarked to him.

'Yeah,' was Averell's reply. 'Just be ready with that Winchester of yours and don't hesitate to shoot first.'

Averell had intended to keep the buckboard going, straight through the bunched group of Durbin and his men if necessary, but he never got the chance. Durbin and his men came on at such a speed that they had grabbed the reins of his horse and brought the buckboard to a halt almost before he knew what had happened. Josh raised his rifle to let off a shot at the man who had grabbed the reins but he was shot dead before he got the butt of it anywhere near his shoulder.

'What the. . . ?' Averell began to ask.

'Shut up, Averell!' Durbin snarled at him, looking about for what he thought might be a suitably strong enough tree. 'Give me the rope,' he said to one of his men, who had it hooked over the horn of his saddle.

A look of horror and panic spread across Averell's face as he realized what Durbm was intending to do with him. He tried to reach for his gun as he was pulled from the

15

driver's seat of the buckboard, but too late.

'You can't do this,' he said, struggling to get free.

'It's exactly what gets done to cattle-thieves,' Durbin replied.

'I ain't stolen anyone's cattle.'

'Shut up,' Durbin snarled. 'Put the noose around his neck and take him to that tree over there with the boulder underneath it.'

Averell was a strong man. He put up a determined struggle but he was no match for the men who were manhandling him. One of them put the noose round his neck and pulled it tight. Then he was dragged by it and shoved on to the boulder under the tree Durbin had chosen to hang him from. Already beginning to choke, he was not able speak another word. One of the men threw the end of the rope over a branch of the tree. Riding up, Durbin caught it and tied it to the horn of his saddle. Then he walked his horse off a distance of a few yards, stopping only when Averell had been hoisted a foot from the boulder and was dangling in the air. Everyone looking on, Durbin included, saw Averell die a horribly cruel death. They all looked on in silence as he kicked and fought against strangulation until at last after some minutes his legs became still and his tongue lolled from his mouth.

'Right,' Durbin said, untying the end of the rope from the horn of his saddle, letting Averell's body drop to the ground. 'Let's go and get the whore.'

'Now?' one of the younger cowpokes asked, not really meaning to. He only just managed not to throw up everything his guts contained at what he'd just witnessed. He literally had no stomach to go through it a second time, especially not with a woman. The others, Durbin included, felt the same but none of them was going to say so until he saw what Durbin's reaction was going to be. Joe South wouldn't have hesitated and they'd have had no choice but to follow. But South wasn't leading them. Durbin was and they knew him to be only half the monster South was.

Durbin thought for a moment or two. Then he said, 'Well, maybe this'll frighten her into realizing Bosworth means business.'

The others didn't say it out loud but they were all happy to agree with him.

'All right,' he said. 'Let's get the hell out of here.'

*

The rest of the day went by. No one came down the old Oregon Trail to discover the gory remains of Jim Averell and at the roadhouse Ellie Watson went about the day's business of running the place. She worried about Jim and hoped he'd be all right. As the day wore on she began to expect him back anytime. Then, as dusk began to fall, she did begin to worry and decided to go and seek out O'Brien, who was outside tending to the livestock. She found him by the cattle pens.

'Mick,' she said to him, 'I'm worried about Jim. He should be back by now.'

O'Brien looked at the sun, which had already sunk low in the sky. Then he looked down the track along which Averell and Josh would be riding home.

'Maybe they got delayed,' he replied, trying to hide his own concern at their lateness.

'You don't think. . . ?' Ellie began.

'Not in town, Ellie. Bothwell wouldn't try anything there. Give them another hour. If they're not back by then maybe I'll start to worry.'

'I gotta a bad feeling about it,' Ellie replied.

O'Brien knew how much in love she and Averell were and guessed she was bound to be feeling fretful.

'He's got Josh with him,' he said, trying to reassure her. 'And look how he stood up to Bothwell's men in the roadhouse yesterday. He's more than a match for anyone and I think it's a well-known fact. Besides, he's a justice of the peace now. That means something in the county and Bothwell knows it.'

Ellie said nothing but the look on her face told O'Brien she wasn't convinced. He would have liked to tell her he'd saddle up and go down the trail and look for them but his job was to stay put and look after her. He decided he had to tell her this.

'Ellie, you know Jim wanted me to stay and watch out for things here, but maybe, if he and Josh don't show up in the next hour or so, we could send one of the boys down the trail to look for them.'

'All right,' Ellie replied. 'But I am worried, Mick. Very worried.'

And with that she turned and walked back to the house.

19

THREE

Durbin arrived back at Bothwell's spread, the Round Circle ranch, knowing he had to report back to him. What was he going to tell him? That they'd hanged both of them? He could do that but it wouldn't be long before Bothwell knew it was a lie and then he'd be in trouble. And, as Averell had just discovered, trouble was not something you wanted to get into with a man like Bothwell. He'd told the others to say nothing to anyone. It was not something the world was supposed to know about anyway, so he reckoned he could count on them to keep quiet. But it was Bothwell's business and it couldn't really be kept from him.

He walked his mount to the stables.

Lynch a woman? The horror of the thought would not leave him. Then he had an idea. Why didn't he go and talk to Ellen Watson himself, alone, and try and persuade her that now, if she wanted to save her own life, she had only one choice? To take whatever Bothwell had offered her and Averell for their homesteads and get out of the county. Surely once she found out what had happened to Averell she'd be frightened into realizing she had no other choice. Once she knew? Knew what? That it was he who'd hanged her lover? A cattle-thief, he quickly reminded himself. They were both cattle-thieves and he had to make her see that if she wasn't careful she'd suffer the same fate as her lover. This was the answer, he decided: to try and make her see sense. As a woman, he at least owed her that. To this end, he decided to ride out to the roadhouse. If she chose to ignore his advice, then – well, she probably would end up getting hanged. If not by him, then, he guessed by the law, woman or no woman. Bothwell was power-ful enough to ensure that.

It was dark now and Jim and Josh had not returned from town. Mick O'Brien informed

Ellie that he was going to send one of the boys to look for them. He chose a young cowpoke named Jerry Wheeler.

'You'll come across them, no doubt, on the trail. If you do ride straight back and tell us. And if for some reason they're staying the night in town, ride back and tell us that, too,' he instructed him, as Wheeler swung up on to his horse.

'Sure thing,' Wheeler replied before spurring his horse into a gallop.

'Thank God the moon's pretty full,' Ellie said to O'Brien, as they both watched Wheeler disappear.

'Yeah,' O'Brien replied, pensively. Like Ellie, he had begun to have a bad feeling about things, though he tried not to let it show.

'I suppose I'd better get back to the house,' Ellie said wearily. 'There's already a good crowd in there.'

A tough character and a natural inclination to hope for the best was all that was keeping her going. O'Brien had always held her in high esteem and his heart went out to her as he watched her walk away. Seeing her climb the steps to the entrance to the roadhouse, he turned and went to do the rounds of the men he'd placed at various look-out positions to make sure they were still being vigilant in keeping an eye out for a return of Bothwell's men.

The first thing Jerry Wheeler came across as he rode down the Oregon Trail was the buckboard and pretty quickly after that Josh's dead body lying beside it. What there didn't appear to be any sign of was his boss, Jim Averell. He looked all around the buckboard for a body but at first he didn't see anything. Then he began to notice a mess of horseshoe prints in the dirt. As he examined them he was led to the boulder and the tree that had served as the gallows on which Averell had been hanged.

'Oh my God!' he said out loud, as he took in the gruesome sight of Averell's murdered body. And not just the body, but the evidence that wild critters had already been making a meal of it. Seconds later he was vomiting violently.

His first thought as he began to collect himself was to hurry back to the roadhouse and tell O'Brien but then he realized he couldn't just leave Averell and Josh where they were to be further devoured by wild animals. He had to get them both on to the buckboard and take them home. He managed to achieve this, but not without more retching brought on by a level of revulsion life had never given him the experience of knowing before. A young cowpoke had suddenly had to become a man.

The journey back to the roadhouse seemed to take for ever. It was nearly midnight when he at last pulled the buckboard to a halt by the front steps. He knew there would still be a number of revellers enjoying themselves inside. He could hear them, and he wondered how he was going to be able to step in there and tell Ellen Watson what had happened to her lover Jim Averell. He was, though, to be saved the misery of the task. For as he began to climb down from the buckboard Mick O'Brien suddenly appeared. O'Brien came from the horse end of it and had not seen the gruesome cargo carried in the back.

'Find anything?' O'Brien asked.

The young cowpoke was never more relieved in his life to see anyone, as he was then to see O'Brien.

'Oh God, Mick!' he said. 'They killed them.'

'What d'you mean?' O'Brien asked. Even though it was what he'd half-expected to hear, his blood ran cold and his voice showed it. 'When? Where?'

'A few miles down the road. They shot Josh and hanged Jim,' Wheeler replied, stepping to the side of the buckboard and indicating with a pointed forefinger where the corpses of both men lay.

'The bastards!' O'Brien cursed through clenched teeth. 'The dirty, low-down bastards!'

The words had barely escaped his mouth, when the door of the roadhouse opened and out stepped Ellen Watson.

'Mick, is that you?' she called out on seeing the buckboard at the bottom of the steps.

Although there was plenty of moonlight it was still difficult to see things clearly from even a small distance.

'Is Jerry back? Are they OK?' she asked, stepping forward and peering into the night.

O'Brien didn't know how to answer her. But from the top of the roadhouse steps looking down Ellie couldn't fail to see that there were two bodies in the back of the buckboard.

'Oh no,' she groaned, putting a hand to her mouth to stifle a sob. 'Oh no!'

O'Brien was afraid she was going to faint and he stepped forward to catch her. But, as he should have known, Ellie Watson was made of sterner stuff than that. Though her heart was breaking at what she knew was the unavoidable truth, she had to step forward to confirm it to herself. As she came down the steps O'Brien stepped aside and let her reach the buckboard. Jim's tongue was still protruding from his mouth and, though Wheeler had removed the rope from around his neck, she could see that he had been hanged.

'Where? When?' she asked in angry tones.

O'Brien let Wheeler tell his story. When he had finished the three of them were silent for a time, staring into the buckboard. Though her heart was broken, Ellie was trying to collect herself. She was finding it hard to control her breathing and she would like to have fallen into O'Brien's arms and let her grief flow. But she knew she had to be strong. Not just for her own and everyone else's sake but because... of Jim. Bothwell had done this terrible thing. Of this she had no doubt. And he was going to pay. God, how he was going to pay! Even now, so soon, as she looked down on the gruesome sight of her lover's broken body, which had been preyed upon by man and beast alike, she swore to avenge his murder.

'Take them to the barn,' she instructed O'Brien. 'We'll send for Preacher Jones and bury them both in the morning.'

Then she turned and climbed the steps to go back into the roadhouse, leaving Wheeler and O'Brien to be overawed by her composure. They did not know though, that as they led the horse and buckboard to the barn, Ellie had gone straight to the bedroom she and Jim Averell had shared. There she had fallen on to the bed and sobbed, until at last, forlorn and exhausted, she had fallen asleep.

FOUR

Durbin, who had successfully avoided coming up against Bothwell, had spent the night in the bunkhouse. He had saddled his horse and was getting ready to ride out to the roadhouse to talk to Ellen Watson, when Bothwell's foreman came up to him and told him his boss wanted to see him.

'What, now?' Durbin asked, impatience and unease showing in his voice.

'Yeah,' was all the foreman said in reply, turning and walking away.

Word of Averell's hanging had, of course, got around and Bothwell's ranch hands' minds were concentrated on it. Most reckoned Bothwell was powerful enough to get away with it, but they also knew that only half of the job had been done. This was

Durbin's fault and they all knew Bothwell would have something to say about it. They all waited to see exactly what.

Durbin tied up his horse and walked over to the ranch house. He found Bothwell in his office and by the look on his face knew he was in for trouble.

'Come in and shut the door,' Bothwell said to him impatiently.

Durbin's hand had barely let go of the door handle, when Bothwell snapped at him, 'Your instructions were to hang both of them.'

'Averell was on his own. We came across him driving a buckboard into town,' was Durbin's reasoned reply.

'I know,' replied Bothwell. 'But why didn't you ride on to the roadhouse and hang her?'

'Because,' Durbin, though without meaning to, suddenly found himself saying, 'She's a woman, Mr Bothwell, and it don't come easy to a man to stretch a woman's neck.'

Bothwell looked at him for a moment. He had barely a thread of decency in him, especially when it came to the ruthlessness with which he was trying to build up a cattleman's empire, but even he could see Durbin's point. Before he could say anything in reply, Durbin added:

'I thought I'd try one more time to frighten her. Maybe the death of Averell would make her finally see sense and she'd agree to sell.'

'And if it doesn't?'

'She's a cattle-thief, ain't she?' was Durbin's reply.

'She was a cattle-thief yesterday,' Bothwell remarked.

He wasn't any longer convinced that Durbin was man enough to finish the job he had been given.

'Look, Durbin, if you ain't got the stomach to finish this, just say so, and I'll get some-one else to do it. When I give an order I expect it to be carried out to the letter, or else.'

'I don't like cattle-thieves any more than the next man, Mr Bothwell,' Durbin replied firmly, 'and if Ellen Watson don't see that we mean to stop her once and for all, then she'll pay the price for it. But I didn't see the harm in giving her one more warning.'

'OK, Durbin, but I want this job finished today. Either that woman agrees to sell her and Averell's land to me or she dies. Have you got that? This thing's in danger of getting out of hand and, if it does, I'll hold you personally responsible.'

Anyone overhearing their conversation could have been forgiven for thinking the two men were talking at cross-purposes but they'd have been wrong. Cattle-thieving was the excuse Bothwell was using to justify his murderous actions, but both men knew there was no real proof that Ellen Watson and Jim Averell had stolen anyone's cattle. It was just a ruse to get hold of their land and the stretch of river Bothwell needed to water his livestock.

'It'll be done, Mr Bothwell,' Durbin said.

'Good,' Bothwell replied, in a tone of voice that told him he was dismissed.

As Durbin turned to leave and had his hand on the doorknob, Bothwell added, 'And don't forget, you'll also be ridding the county of that den of iniquity they call a roadhouse.'

Durbin made no reply. Instead he threw Bothwell a look that told him he'd already made his point. Then he pulled open the door and was gone.

'I'll expect you back here later,' Bothwell called after him.

By now word had reached town of what had happened to Jim Averell. Casper was still a small town but it had a sheriff, a man who perhaps, it was said, was only reluctantly in the pay of the Wyoming Stock Growers' Association. Averell had been a justice of the peace and was looked upon as a good citizen of the county. Sheriff Hal Conner appeared genuinely appalled to hear of what had happened to him and he decided to take a few men and ride out to the road-house. They arrived a few hours after Averell's and Josh's funeral. Preacher Jones had carried out the service and neighbours and friends had attended. They were all gathered in the roadhouse when the sheriff and his men arrived.

'I'm sorry for your loss, ma'am,' Conner said to Ellie, walking up to her and taking off his hat.

Ellie thanked him and then asked him what he was going to do about it.

'Do you know exactly what happened?' the sheriff asked her.

'No, but I think we can all guess,' was her reply.

'Who found the bodies?'

'Jerry Wheeler,' Mick O'Brien, who was

33

standing in a group surrounding Ellie, spoke up. 'Didn't you, son,' he added, turning to Wheeler.

'Tell me about it,' Conner instructed him. 'All I've heard so far is gossip and rumour.'

'It was Bothwell,' Ellie interjected. 'His men got Jim on the trail and they lynched him.'

'Did anyone see it happen?' Sheriff Conner asked.

'Josh maybe did but they shot him. Before or after we'll never know,' Ellie replied. She was still in a state of shock and the tone of her voice showed it. Nevertheless, she was still managing to put up a good front and everyone was admiring her for it.

'Without witnesses . . .' Sheriff Conner began to say, but he was cut short by Ellie saying.

'Bothwell did it and everyone knows, witnesses or no. He's been wanting my and Jim's land long enough and plenty of people have been witness to that.'

Sheriff Conner knew she was right. Averell had only recently spoken to him about it and they had both discussed their fears about the lengths Bothwell would go to get it.

'Well, I'll go and see him, Miss Watson, but I can guess what his reaction will be. As I said, without witnesses we ain't got nothing on him.'

'And,' O'Brien chipped in cynically, 'we all know he's a member of the Wyoming Stock Growers' Association and no one messes with them and gets away with it.'

'Yeah,' other voices were heard to mutter in agreement.

'No one's above the law,' Sheriff Conner tried to reassure them, but they all felt they knew differently and dismissed his remarks accordingly.

'Well, there'll be an inquest held and people will be able to have their say then. Are you sure Jim was hanged? You shouldn't have buried him, you know, until the law had certified how he died.'

'He was hanged all right,' Mick O'Brien insisted. 'Preacher Jones here can testify to that, as can the rest of us.'

'I sure can,' the preacher agreed.

'But neither he nor any of you are a doctor and only a doctor can formally record the cause of a death. You should all have known that. You in particular, Preacher.'

'Well, dig them up, then,' Ellie suddenly

declared. 'The beasts of the field have already made a meal of them. The worms won't have had a chance yet to have done much more damage.'

Everyone was shocked by what she suggested but Sheriff Conner declared that maybe they had no choice. Someone official had to say how Jim and Josh had died. Mick O'Brien said he'd open up the graves. Conner said he'd take the bodies into town and that they could be reburied the next day.

'Well, I ain't ever heard the like of it,' Preacher Jones said, hoping to comfort Ellie, as O'Brien, with some of the ranch hands and Sheriff Conner and his men, left the roadhouse to do their grisly work.

'It don't matter none,' Ellie said, 'if it helps nail Bothwell.'

She harboured no illusions that it would but that didn't matter to her. She was already formulating her own plans for making Bothwell pay for what he had done.

FIVE

It was quickly certified by a doctor in Casper, the town to which Jim Averell and Josh Abbott had been heading, just how the two men had met their deaths. There was still no real proof that Bothwell had had a hand in it but everyone in town knew it could be no one else. Especially Sheriff Conner. He, though, owed his job to the Wyoming Stock Growers' Association and he didn't feel inclined to go laying blame for anything at the feet of one of its most prominent members, when in reality it was they who were the law around those parts. But he had to be seen to at least be trying to do his job and he participated fully in a quickly-convened inquest into their deaths. Under the auspices of an acting coroner, justice of the peace B.F. Emery, a seven-man jury confirmed the obvious, while declaring that the hanging and the shooting were carried out by a person or persons unknown. This was followed immediately by a campaign in the town's newspaper, which was, not surprisingly, also controlled by the Association, to discredit Jim Averell as a ruthless criminal who had robbed Sweetwater Valley ranchers for years. Ellen Watson, it was claimed, was not only his accomplice but she also kept a whorehouse. It was added that Sweetwater Valley would be all the sweeter if she had suffered the same fate as Averell.

Ellen Watson had remained at the roadhouse when Jim Averell's and Josh Abbott's bodies were dug up and taken to town. Mick O'Brien travelled with them but he had left what he thought were able-enough ranch hands to watch out for their mistress. Bothwell was, however, not expected to act again so soon and no one thought she was in any particular or imminent danger. This mean that when Henry Durbin walked into the roadhouse not long after Mick O'Brien and Sheriff Conner had started for Casper with their gruesome cargo he did so unchallenged.

Ellie recognized him immediately as being a member of the gang Joe South had brought into the roadhouse only two days before.

'You've got a nerve coming here after what's happened,' she said to him as he walked up to the bar.

'Ma'am, I don't know nothing about what's happened or who's responsible for it,' he lied. 'I just came here to tell you that it needn't happen to you.'

Ellie was standing behind the bar and she knew that under it within easy reach was a shotgun. Grief-stricken and broken hearted though she was, her first inclination was to grab it. But she knew the big iron hanging at Durbin's side would be out and threatening her before she could get to it. People out West didn't usually strike down women in cold blood but equally she knew she couldn't count on any decency or honour where Bothwell was concerned.

'I suppose Bothwell sent you here to tell me that, did he?' she said instead.

Hearing her words, Durbin couldn't help but be impressed by the unbending bravery of them. There were half a dozen cowboys in the roadhouse, all armed, but he didn't feel that any of them was half the man she was. None so far had stood up to make a show of solidarity with her. They were all just waiting to see what happened. He decided on a more conciliatory approach.

'Look, Miss Watson,' he said to her.

'No,' she interrupted him. 'You look. My and Jim's land ain't for sale, at any price. Even Jim's death. Now you can go back and tell Bothwell that or you can stay here and find it out for yourself.'

'And you think he'll listen now any more than he did before?' Durbin replied, still trying to keep his tone of voice reasonable rather than threatening.

'I don't care,' Ellie said.

She would have said more but a young cowboy who was a customer spoke up for her.

'Can't a lady even be allowed to grieve over the murder of someone she loved?'

Durbin looked around to where the voice had come from to see to whom it belonged.

'You'd best stay out of what ain't none of your business,' he said to the cowboy, his right hand tensing above his gun.

Quick as a flash, while his eyes were off her, Ellie grabbed the shotgun that was under the bar and pulling back both triggers aimed it at him. Durbin knew it was too late to draw.

'Well, now . . .' he began to say but before he could get out any more words the young cowboy got to his feet and drawing his own gun walked up to him.

'You don't seem to be getting the message,' he said, taking Durbin's gun out of its holster, throwing open the cylinder and emptying its bullets on to the floor.

'And what message would that be?' Durbin asked.

'That my and Jim's land ain't for sale,' Ellie reminded him.

'Now get out of here or I'm gonna throw you out,' the cowboy told him, holding his gun for him to claim back, if he so chose.

Durbin knew he was beaten.

'All right,' he said, 'but this ain't gonna be the last of it, which is all I came here to tell you.'

He had barely got the words out when the air around him was filled with a thunderous noise and pieces of plaster began to fall on him from the ceiling above. Both he and

41

the cowboy stepped back in shock. Both, though, stood their ground, as they turned to see Ellie standing with the barrels of the shotgun smoking.

Durbin knew he had better go while he still could. Snatching his gun from out of the young cowboy's hand, he took hurried but measured footsteps towards the door. As he got to it, he stopped as if to say something, but didn't. Instead he kicked the door open, walked through it and was gone.

'I should have just killed him,' Ellie remarked. She lowered the shotgun and dropped it on to the bar. 'Thank you,' she said to the young cowboy.

She would have said more but suddenly all the grief she felt over the murder of Jim welled up inside her. Bringing up a hand to stifle a sob, she turned and ran into a room behind the bar. She shut the door behind her and let the tears flow. As they did so, the cowboy returned to his seat to finish his beer.

SIX

Albert Bothwell, who was standing looking out of a window in his office, was happy with the findings of the inquest into Jim Averell's murder. It was the way the jury was supposed to see things. Payments to Sheriff Conner had seen to that. What he was not happy about was Durbin's failure to deal with Ellie Watson. He should have gone on to the homestead and hanged her after he'd dealt with Averell. It would have been simple and the matter would already by now have been on the way to becoming history. Joe South would not have hung about, getting squeamish about things. He'd have got the job done. But Joe was out of it now. A right hand short, his gun-toting days were over.

Such were the thoughts that were running through his mind, when one of his men came into his office.

'What is it, Jack?' Bothwell asked him.

'Just heard a rumour about Durbin,' Jack Green replied.

'Ain't he back yet?'

'No. But I just heard he went to the road-house on his own and got bested there by Ellie Watson and some cowpoke who stood up for her. Came pretty close, they're saying, to getting shot.'

'What?' Bothwell questioned in exasperated tones. 'Where is he?'

'Well, he ain't come back yet.'

Green, who'd never liked Durbin much, was pleased to be bringing damning news about him to his boss.

'What is wrong with the man?' Bothwell snarled. 'And why ain't he come back yet?'

'Supposed to be something to do with the fact that she's a woman,' Green said.

'Yeah, a cattle-rustling whore of a woman,' Bothwell replied scathingly. 'Any woman that rustles cattle, especially my cattle, has got a man's punishment coming to her. Anyway, what were the others doing when Durbin was busy nearly

44

getting himself shot?'

'Nothing,' Green replied. 'He didn't take no one with him. Rumour is he just walked into the bar and tried to talk her into believing it was in her best interests to sell you their homesteads.'

'God damnit!' Bothwell snarled. 'The time for that is over, as he well knows.'

Green didn't say anything but just let his boss express his anger and indignation over the failure of Durbin to carry out his orders as directed. Then he remarked:

'If Durbin ain't come back yet, maybe he ain't going to.'

Such a pronouncement made Bothwell stop and think. Then he declared:

'Well, if no one around here is capable of finishing what has to be done, then I guess I'll have to do it myself.'

His words left Green a little crestfallen. He'd hoped Bothwell would pass the job on to him.

'Well, maybe I and some of the boys could go over to the roadhouse . . .' he began to say but was interrupted by Bothwell saying:

'And what?'

Green didn't answer right away.

'Exactly,' Bothwell said. 'The opportunity has passed. It's too late now. Folks might not have questioned too deeply the killing of the pair of them, but they would now question the hanging of her. Nah, she's gotta die some other way.'

As he said it Bothwell turned away from Green to look out of his office window. It gave him a view of his acreage. He needed the access to the river that Watson's and Averell's land would give him, if he were to consolidate his cattle-ranching empire. He had to have that land and no damned woman was going to stand in the way of his getting it.

'Go back to your work,' he said to Green without turning around. 'Just go back to your work.'

It wasn't the way Green wanted the conversation with his boss to end but he knew better than to labour the point further.

'And if Durbin returns send him straight to me,' Bothwell said to him, still looking out of the window.

'Sure thing, boss,' Green replied, leaving.

Durbin was not, though, going to be returning. The qualms he'd had about dealing with Ellie Watson the way Bothwell wanted him to, were compounded by the gallantry the young cowpoke in the roadhouse had shown in taking her part and standing up to him. He realized that if he were going to be involved in the affair at all, it was not going to be on the side of Bothwell. Killing Jim Averell was one thing. That was just dog eat dog. But killing a woman, that was something else. And he couldn't do it. Not to satisfy the greedy ambitions of a man like Bothwell. He wanted now to be on Ellen Watson's side. That was what the actions of the young cowboy had revealed to him. The only question now was how to achieve it. As he rode away from the roadhouse, he decided he needed time to think on it. He couldn't go back to Bothwell's, that was obvious. Instead, he decided, he'd spend some time on the range thinking about things. Meantime, he reckoned, Ellen Watson was in safe enough hands. The young cowboy, whoever he was, wasn't going to let anything happen to her.

Indeed he wasn't, but who was he? Ellie Watson herself pondered the question as she sat forlornly in the back room drying her tears and struggling to come to terms with the loss of her lover. She had seen him in the bar on occasions but had thought of him as just another cowboy blow-in from the surrounding ranch lands wetting his whistle. He had not stood out particularly and was not one of the crowd who made up the regulars of the place. But yet it was he and not they who had come to her aide in her time of need. She thought, pulling herself together, that she should go and thank him and, at the very least, let him drink on the house. But when she went to find him he had gone.

'Who was that?' she asked of the regular barkeep, Bart Jackson.

'You mean the young cowboy?' Jackson asked her.

When Ellie said yes he said that he didn't know but that he'd been in a few times.

'Well, next time he comes in, give him a drink on the house and let me know he's here,' Ellie said.

Then she went to what had been her own and Jim Averell's living-quarters. She could have wished the young cowboy had not left the roadhouse – she would have felt safer knowing he was about – but equally she supposed there was no reason why he should become any more involved in her fight with Bothwell.

SEVEN

As it became more apparent to Bothwell that Durbin was not coming back he became more and more irate. Durbin was someone he had thought he *could* count on. Indeed after Joe South he was the only other person he felt he could count upon. Without either of the two men he knew he was going to have to do the job himself and this was not something he felt he could risk being seen to do. As a member of the Wyoming Stock Growers' Association he couldn't afford to be seen to be adopting murderous tactics to secure his business, though everyone knew it was how ranching empires were carved out of the virgin lands of America. But he had to get rid of that woman and get rid of her now, before she became too much of a *cause célèbre* in the county, if not the territory.

As he paced up and down his office wondering what to do, he began to realize that he had no choice but to re-enlist the services of Joe South. He knew that he was about the ranch somewhere recovering from having lost his right hand. He decided to send for Jack Green to go find him. Green found him in one of the bunkhouses on the ranch. When told that the boss wanted to see him, South, who had been miserable, assuming his days of usefulness were over, suddenly perked up and hurried along to Bothwell's office.

'How's the arm, Joe?' Bothwell asked him by way of greeting as he entered his office.

'It's healing but the hand still feels as if it's there,' was South's reply.

'Good, good,' Bothwell remarked.

'I've been practising with the left but it ain't the same though,' said South, wondering where the small talk was leading to, knowing it was not something his boss usually indulged in.

'No, I don't suppose it is and it will take time.'

'What did you want to see me about, boss?' South asked, keen to know if he was thought still to be of some use to Bothwell.

'It's the Averell and Watson business,' Bothwell replied. 'You've probably heard it ain't been satisfactorily concluded yet.'

'I had heard talk,' South said, taking his right arm in his left hand and holding it a few inches beneath the stump. Talk of the Averell business was a stark reminder to him of what he took to be the cruel fate that had befallen him.

'Yeah, well, Durbin only did half the job and not the greater part of it. And now he's disappeared, leaving the Watson whore still stubbornly in possession of their acreage.'

'Well, what's to be done about it?' South asked, still cradling his stump in his good hand as if it was paining him.

Noticing that he was doing so, Bothwell, putting on a show of concern, asked him to excuse his lack of courtesy and told him to sit down.

'Well,' he went on to say, 'that depends on you. Durbin seems to be out of the picture now and there ain't nobody else I can trust to finish the job that's been started.'

South thought for a moment, looking

down at the bloodstained bandage wrapped around the stump of what used to be his shooting hand.

'I don't see as I can be of much use,' he said to Bothwell.

'The men all respect you, Joe, and you know how to lead them. And this time there'll be no pussyfooting about.'

'What have you got in mind then?' South asked, suddenly feeling full of stature and still of some worth after all.

'Burning her out,' Bothwell said, coming straight to the point. 'The roadhouse, the barns, every last building they've got. And then driving off her livestock.'

South thought for a moment and then asked, 'And if she puts up any resistance?'

'Kill her. Kill them all,' Bothwell replied firmly. 'It's the only way. This matter has got to be settled once and for all.'

'It's what should have happened sooner,' South remarked, lifting his stump and adding, 'maybe then this wouldn't have happened.'

'Yeah, well, don't worry about that,' Bothwell reassured him. 'I'll see you're all right after.'

'When do you want it done?' South asked,

being too macho to easily accept sympathy from Bothwell.

'Now. Today,' Bothwell replied resolutely.

'Right,' South said, getting up from the chair his boss had invited him to sit in.

There was no more to be said and he turned to leave.

'Do it right,' Bothwell said to him in earnest tones.

'You don't have to worry about that,' said South, looking back. 'Someone's gotta pay for this,' he added, again holding up the stump of his right arm.

After he'd gone Bothwell wished he had also told him to hunt down Durbin and deal with him, but he supposed that this was something South would take upon himself to do anyway should the opportunity arise.

EIGHT

The bodies of Jim Averell and Josh Abbott had been released into the care of Mick O'Brien and he and Jerry Wheeler, accompanied by the preacher, had brought them back to the roadhouse for reinternment.

'So Bothwell goes scot free,' was all Ellie Watson said by way of comment to them when they returned.

'Maybe,' was O'Brien's response. Next he asked, 'We gonna rebury Jim and Josh now?'

'Guess so,' Ellie replied.

Everyone thought again how remarkably well she was bearing up to things.

Mick O'Brien was soon informed of Durbin's visit and the young cowboy's gallantry in standing up for Ellie. Expressing relief that the cowboy had at least been there to help her, he cursed their own men for not having acted.

'They were all keeping a look-out for trouble outside,' Ellie said in their defence. 'No one expected trouble inside. Besides, Durbin came alone and it wasn't immediately obvious who he was.'

O'Brien wasn't convinced it was excuse enough but dropped the matter to get on with the business of reburying Averell and Abbott. It was, if anything, more solemn an occasion than the previous burial. The shock of their murders had given way to grief and Ellie felt her heart would break even more over the loss of the man she loved and had planned to spend the rest of her life with. Mick O'Brien watched her. His heart went out to her and he wondered what she was going to do now. He thought she should sell the roadhouse and both homesteads but he knew she wouldn't. She would hang on, to the bitter end, if that's what it meant. Well, he thought to himself, he'd remain at her side, even if it meant giving up his own life to defend hers.

They sang a last hymn and Preacher Jones said his last words. Then they filed back to the roadhouse. The regular barkeep took up his place behind the bar and poured them all a drink.

'Thank you, Solomon, for conducting the service all over again,' Ellie said to the preacher.

'Thank me not, Ellie, my dear. But thank the Lord.'

And so saying the preacher sank a shot of whiskey. He was a tall and stocky bewhiskered man whom everyone admired for being a man of the world as much as a man of God.

'Well,' he asked, after sinking a second shot of whiskey, 'what are you going to do now, Ellie?'

'Carry on as before,' was Ellie's reply.

'Do you think that's possible?' Solomon asked her.

Ellie looked around her before replying. Business had been quiet for the few days that had passed since Jim and Josh had been murdered. The girls had been discreet and the customers had not made so much play for them. But she knew things would now start to return to normal and the place would soon be humming again with people having a good time of it.

'It's what Jim would have wanted,' Ellie replied, feeling a lump come to her throat as she said it. But pulling herself together, she added, 'And besides, Bothwell ain't gonna win.'

'Hasn't he already won?' the preacher asked. His tone of voice was not defeatest but tender and Ellie knew he was simply looking out for her.

Ellie again felt a lump rising in her throat. Joining her hands together in prayer fashion and bringing them up to her face, she replied:

'Maybe that's why I ain't going nowhere. To show him that he ain't won. I love this place as much as I loved Jim. There was nothing here when Jim and I staked our claims to this land and what there is now we built up between us by the sweat of our brows. Why should we let someone like Bothwell drive us off?'

'Because he's the power in the land. You know that.'

'No,' said Ellie firmly. 'He might think he is but he ain't. The law is. Jim was. He was a justice of the peace. He was formally appointed so by the judiciary. Bothwell is nothing, except a greedy, land grabbing sonofabitch who I am gonna cut down to size.'

Ellie's tone had gone from one of firmness to anger and everyone stood back in shock as they heard her.

'Are you gonna cut down to size the whole of the Wyoming Stock Growers' Association, then? Because that's what you're going to have to do, if you're going to get Bothwell,' Solomon told her, pushing his empty shot-glass forward for the barkeep to refill.

'If that's what it takes,' was her reply.

Looking at her, Solomon knew she meant it. The papers and the gossips of the town and the county beyond had labelled her a whore and they claimed that the roadhouse was nothing more than a brothel. She and Jim had stood up to that and besides, the rest of the folk knew that what she and Jim were doing was providing a public service and one that played its part in keeping the world safe and decent for respectable, God-fearing folk to live in. They were happy to turn a blind eye to the roadhouse's existence, as long as it didn't impinge upon their own lives.

But the ordinary folk didn't really have the power to change things and were, besides, too busy trying in what was still a harsh environment to survive. With the Wyoming Stock Growers' Association, though, it was a different matter. Preacher Jones had witnessed this enough from first hand to know they really were the power in the land and that they trampled to death anyone who got in the way of their ambitions.

'You know they say you steal their stock and rebrand it as your own,' he said to her.

'Sure I do,' Ellie replied.

'Well, whether you do or not, that's the excuse Bothwell uses for coming after you.'

'Maybe, but everyone knows the real reason.'

'That doesn't make any difference. He'll still get away with it.'

'Not while I live and breathe,' Ellie informed him between gritted teeth.

'That's what worries me, Ellie, my dear. That's what worries me,' Solomon remarked in tones that matched his name.

'Well, you don't have to worry, Preacher,' Mick O'Brien suddenly chipped in. 'Not while me and the boys are here. We'll protect her.'

And you'll all die, just like Jim and Josh, the preacher wanted to reply but he knew it

62

would be cruel to do so. Beside which, if Ellie was going to stay and put up a fight, he wanted them to be at her side. He didn't want to frighten anyone off. So, instead he said:

'I know you will. Just be careful.'

He might have advised them not to take the law into their own hands. But, since Bothwell and his friends in the Wyoming Stock Growers' Association had done just that, he knew he'd be wasting his time. Sheriff Conner was a good man and he kept the peace well enough in Casper, but he was no match for the bigger battles that were being fought in the county and that was really all there was to it.

'Well, just be careful,' he said. 'Just be careful.'

Then, making the shotglass of whiskey Bart had put down in front of him his last he got up to leave.

' Whatever folks say, Ellie, I know you're a good woman,' he added.

'Thank you, Solomon,' Ellie said, walking with him to the door.

'I'll pray for you,' were Solomon's last words to her, as he climbed into his buggy and rode off.

Watching him go, Ellie thought of what a good man of the Lord he really was. He and Jim had been good friends and she knew that his fears for her were genuine.

'Yeah,' she said to herself, thinking of his last words. 'Please do that. Because I know I'm going to need it.'

NINE

It was dark a few hours after the preacher
had ridden away and riding on to the homestead came Joe South and half a dozen of
the Round Circle ranch's men. The Round
Circle was the name of Bothwell's ranch
and the men had left there fully equipped
with kerosene-soaked torches and even
some sticks of dynamite.

'Right,' said Joe South, 'get the torches
out and get them lit.'

He had no compunction about going up
against a woman. He had convinced himself
she was low-life and was prepared to
pretend he had the kind of morals that a
whore could offend.

'Jack, you stick by me. You're going to act

as my right hand. When I tell you to light the dynamite you light it and I'll throw it.'

'Sure thing, Joe,' was Jack's reply.

'The rest of you set fire to the buildings and make sure they burn good. Shoot anyone who comes running out of them. And shoot to kill. Have you all got that?'

They all answered that they had.

'Right, then, let's go and have us some fun,' South sang out, kicking his horse into a gallop and holding the reins high with his good hand.

As they neared the roadhouse he put his left hand into a saddle-bag and pulled out a stick of dynamite. While his men threw their torches onto the roofs of the roadhouse and other of the homestead buildings, South held out the stick of dynamite for Jack to light. Jack pulled a match from a waistcoat pocket, struck it on his jeans and put it to the fuse of the dynamite stick.

The arrival of Joe South and his men had not gone unnoticed by two men whom Mick O'Brien had ordered to keep watch. But they were young and bored and wishing they could be in the roadhouse where things were beginning to return to normal and people were in there having a good time. They were sharing a smoke and talking when South and his men came riding up. The element of surprise gave South and his men the advantage and the roofs of the buildings were already beginning to burn before the two men were able to grab their Winchesters and let off a few shots.

Inside the roadhouse Mick O'Brien thought he heard the sound of gunfire above the din of the piano-player and people singing along to the tune that was being played. But he wasn't sure. He decided though that he must go and check. He was approaching the door of the roadhouse when Joe South threw the stick of dynamite Jim had just lit into the doorway. There was a loud explosion as the dynamite exploded and the door and most of the front of the roadhouse was blown in. O'Brien was knocked off his feet and fell to the floor unconscious, as debris fell all around him. Other people sitting or standing near the front of the building suffered the same fate, while those at the bar and nearer the back were simply stunned. Ellie, luckily, was in the back room, which was undamaged and left intact after the explosion.

Joe South looked on, impressed at what

he had achieved. Debris from the explosion had fallen around him and Jack but they were not close enough to suffer any harm. As the roadhouse began to burn and people started to come coughing and limping out of it, he let out a holler of devilish delight. He put his left hand into his saddle-bag to pull out another stick of dynamite. He held the reins of his horse in the crook of his right arm, which he held tightly against his body.

'Come on,' he said to Jack, 'let's go and blow up the barn.'

One of the men O'Brien had put on watch had his Winchester aimed at South and he thought he had him clearly in his sights. But when he fired his shot went wide and South lived to ride the few yards to the barn.

'Light it for me,' South ordered Jack, holding the stick of dynamite out.

A few seconds later, with the fuse near burned down, he threw it into the open doors of the barn, heedless of whether or not there was any livestock in it.

In what was left of the roadhouse the dust began to settle and people began to collect themselves. Ellie had made her way into the bar and in the dim light of the few oil-lamps that still burned she tried to find out what had happened. She soon found Bart, the barkeep, who had not suffered any serious injuries.

'What happened, Bart?' she asked him.

'The front of the building's been blown in,' he quickly informed her between coughs, as he tried to clear his lungs of smoke and dust. By now the roof of the roadhouse was completely on fire. 'We've gotta get out of here before the whole building collapses.'

'Where's Mick?' Ellie asked, looking round what was left of the building, trying to see him.

'I don't know,' Bart replied. 'Come on, we've got to get out of here.'

Others in the roadhouse were having the same thoughts and it wasn't long before people began stumbling, some helping others, some on their own, out of the building and dropping on to the ground in front of it. They were in a sorry plight but it didn't seem to influence Joe South and his men one bit. They charged around on their horses adding to the terror of what had happened by making as much noise as they could.

Ellie had found Mick O'Brien, who was

still unconscious, and was trying to wake him up, but without any success. The roof of the building was burning more furiously than ever and she began to fear that it was going to collapse at any minute. She could run out and save herself but she simply could not persuade herself to abandon Mick. Bart had already left the building, so there was no turning to him for help. What was she going to do? She wasn't the sort to lose her nerve but, looking all around her at the devastation and the pieces of burning timber falling from the ceiling as she fought to breathe in the smoke-filled atmosphere, she began to feel a terrible sense of panic grip her. Get out while you still can, a voice began to scream in her head.

'Come on, Mick, wake up,' she pleaded with O'Brien, slapping his face left and right.

At last, as a heavy beam crashed to the ground in a shower of sparks a few feet from her, O'Brien's eyelids began to flicker.

'Thank God!' Ellie exclaimed.

O'Brien, though, was not recovering full consciousness and more beams began crashing down around him and Ellie. Ellie came to the conclusion that if she didn't save herself now she was doomed.

Outside, South and his men were still wreaking havoc. The two cowboys O'Brien had put on guard duty had long ceased firing at them for fear of hitting their own people and were now simply looking on in horror. As Joe South rode his careless path amongst the dying and injured he knew he had to make sure of one thing before his night's work was finished. He had to make sure Ellen Watson did not survive. But there was no sign of her. The burning buildings gave off plenty of light and he knew he'd know her if he saw her but as he rode around there was no sign of her. Had she died in the explosion, he asked himself?

Then he saw her. Reining his horse around to keep it moving he was suddenly facing the roadhouse. There, coming out of it, he saw a woman he knew to be Ellen Watson struggling to help an injured man stay on his feet. South had been holding a rifle in his left hand and now he raised it to his shoulder in readiness to fire. His aim was not going to be perfect but at such close range it was going to be good enough. But nothing else was going to be, for as his finger began to squeeze the trigger something hot and metallic slammed into his hand, shattering it and making his rifle fall to the ground. Then another bullet slammed into the left side of his neck, knocking him from his horse. The last thing he saw as he began to choke to death without a good hand to try and staunch the blood-flow was Durbin riding in amongst them. Durbin, his outraged mind snarled as the darkness of the devil's end began to overwhelm him, Durbin, you double-crossing sonofabitch!

Durbin had no thoughts for him, though. Instead his thoughts were all for Ellie. He raced up to what was left of the front of roadhouse, jumped off his horse and ran to help her and O'Brien. Ellie was confused as she saw him approach her, rifle in hand. She knew instinctively he was coming to her aid but she didn't know why. He was surely on Bothwell's side.

'Don't worry,' he said to her, 'I'm here to help.'

And it was lucky he was. For just as he got her and O'Brien clear of the roadhouse, it collapsed in a pile of burning timber behind them. The three of them fell to the ground as a rush of smoke and fiery ash blew over them.

South's men had seen him go down Robbed of their leader, they lost their direction and their drive. Some of them even lost their lives. For what had undone them galvanized O'Brien's two cowboys into getting off their butts and into action. They brought their rifles to their shoulders and fired fast and accurately at South's men, forcing those they did not kill to flee.

Durbin had quickly got to his feet. His first thoughts were for Ellie and he was relieved to see she was uninjured. Helping her to her feet, he saw that O'Brien, too, seemed to be OK. Then he heard the sound of the two cowboys' rifle fire and saw some of South's men fall from their horses. He was about to take aim with his own rifle, when he saw the rest hightail it away from the scene and disappear into the darkness surrounding the homestead.

Everyone was relieved to see them go.

'I don't understand,' Ellie said to Durbin, seeing that he remained behind while the others fled.

'Well,' replied Durbin, 'I wasn't with them. When something ain't fair, it ain't fair. I worked for Bothwell but it doesn't mean to say I had to obey every order he gave me. That's how I've come to see things. I've been hanging out on the range not too far from here. I saw the flames and knew it could only be Bothwell's doing and reckoned you'd need some help.'

He didn't know if Ellie knew that it was he who'd hanged her lover, he simply knew he had to make amends to her somehow or other. He was tough enough to brave it out for the time being and had decided in his time out on the range that it was something he'd deal with when the time to do so came.

Ellie looked at him, not entirely convinced, but for the time being was just grateful to him for his timely intervention. He'd probably saved her and O'Brien's lives.

'Well, you came in just the nick of time,' she remarked to him.

'Looks like it,' he said.

'Yeah, well now we've got to see to the injured and sort all this mess out. And someone's gotta go to town and bring back the doctor.'

'And Sheriff Conner,' O'Brien added, getting to his feet and managing to remain upright.

'Yeah,' said Durbin, though wondering what it would be worth. It was nothing Bothwell hanging Averell; why should burning down his property and trying to kill his lover amount to anything more?

'If the law won't make Bothwell pay for this, and I don't see that it will,' Ellie remarked, as if she'd read his mind, 'then I will. He thinks he can come on to our land doing whatever he wants. Well, I'm going to show him that two can play at that game. Someone's gonna have to pay to put all this right and it's gonna be him.'

Somehow both Durbin and O' Brien knew she meant it.

TEN

It wasn't long before the town and the county were gasping with horror at what had happened out at the roadhouse. Bothwell was good at denying any involvement and the Stock Growers' Association were good at dismissing any notion that one of their party could be involved in such outrageously criminal activities. But someone who knew what was the inescapable truth of the matter was Sheriff Conner. Three people had died and a number had been seriously injured; this was something that could not easily be swept under the carpet. This meant that his investigations into the outrage had at least to have the appearance of being determined to identify and bring to book the culprits responsible for it. The main fact material to the investigation was, of course, the involvement of Joe South, who was known to be in the employ of Bothwell.

'What more proof do you need'?' Ellie asked him.

'Well,' replied Conner, as he stood with Ellie, O'Brien and Durbin surveying the burned-out wreck of the roadhouse the morning after, 'it could be construed by some as circumstantial evidence. You know what these lawyers can be like. Unless we can prove beyond a shadow of doubt that Bothwell ordered South to come out here and burn the place down, we're on a hiding to nothing.'

'Durbin?' Ellie remarked, looking at Durbin pointedly.

Durbin had no qualms about implicating his old boss in what had happened but he was painfully aware of the fact that he might be opening a can of worms that could only lead to his own ruin. He couldn't help but feel as he stood amongst the sheriff and the others that what was best for him was to get on his horse and keep on riding until Wyoming was a long way behind him. But, as has been said before, he was full of remorse for what he had done and wanted somehow or other, stupidly or otherwise, to make it up to Ellie.

'Everyone knows,' he began, 'it was Bothwell. He wants access to the river for his cattle and the only way to get it and secure it is for him to somehow or other gain ownership of the rights over the river that belonged to Jim and Ellie here.'

'And?' queried Sheriff Conner. 'I mean you ain't exactly telling us something we didn't already know.'

'So there's your proof,' Durbin replied rather weakly.

'Don't you work for Bothwell?' Conner asked him.

'Used to,' Durbin answered. 'But he was asking me to do things my conscience wouldn't allow me to do.'

Sheriff Conner had been told about how it was Durbin who had come to the rescue the night before and of how it was he who had killed Joe South just as he was aiming his rifle at Ellie and O'Brien.

'What sort of things?'

Durbin didn't want to give a direct answer to the question but reckoned he had no choice. Looking at Ellie and then away from her in the direction of the range, he said:

'I was ordered to use any means necessary to persuade Jim and Ellie to sell Bothwell their combined homesteads.'

'Any means?' Sheriff Conner questioned.

Given that his livelihood was in the gift of the Wyoming Stock Growers' Association, Conner himself wasn't sure that he wanted to hear what Durbin was saying.

'Well,' Durbin began, intending to reveal as little of the truth as would allow him to save his own hide. 'I was told to be threatening. I came here and was precisely that but didn't feel it was the way any self-respecting man should be treating a lady.'

The answer was good enough for Conner.

'And you'd be prepared to say that under oath, if called upon to do so?' he asked Durbin.

But before Durbin could answer, Ellie interrupted emotively, asking, 'And did that mean stringing up Jim?'

'I don't think,' interjected Conner, 'he'd be standing here talking to us now if he'd had anything to do with that.'

As he said it he gave Durbin a pointed look, as if to tell him he was not expected to be any more truthful than he had already been. Grateful for it, Durbin simply replied:

'I told you, I don't hold with terrorizing people.'

'Seems to me,' said Conner, pointing in the direction of Joe South's body with a tilt of his head, ' if anyone was involved in the hanging of Jim it was probably him. Jim had after all blown his shooting-hand off.'

'Whoever put the rope around Jim's neck,' Ellie remarked emphatically, 'they was ordered to do it by Bothwell and he's the man who's gotta pay for it. Now what's gonna be done about it, Sheriff?'

'I'll go and see him and tell him what I know,' was Conner's reply. 'And I'll have to tell him about you,' he added, looking at Durbin.

'And arrest him?' Ellie asked, obviously referring to Bothwell.

When Conner didn't give an immediate reply, Ellie simply scoffed.

'Come on,' she said to O'Brien. 'We've got work to do.'

Conner and Durbin threw one another shifty looks and then Durbin followed Ellie and O'Brien.

'I'll take the bodies of South and the

others into town with me, then,' Conner declared, raising his voice a little to make sure he was heard.

He didn't get any reaction from the others, though. Ellie had heard but wasn't interested. She was deep in thought about other things, as was more than obvious to both Durbin and O'Brien.

ELEVEN

Sheriff Conner knew he had to pay a visit to Albert Bothwell. For appearances' sake, if nothing else. He was nervous though. Things were not going to plan. Like Jim Averell, Ellie Watson should have been dead by now. It would then have been an open and shut case and people would have soon forgotten about it. But Ellie Watson was still alive. And what was more, in Henry Durbin she had a very capable man on her side. He would have liked to spoil that budding alliance by telling Ellie Watson exactly what he knew about Durbin's part in the murder of her lover. But how could he without giving himself away? People might guess he was in the pocket of Albert Bothwell, but no one could prove it and he had to make sure it remained that way.

He found Bothwell in what was now becoming his habitual state: exasperation with the way things were going.

'And what do you want?' Bothwell snarled at him when he came before his presence in his office at the Round Circle ranch.

'Things are getting a mite tricky, if you don't mind me saying,' Conner remarked to him, turning his Stetson round in his hands.

'You don't say,' remarked Bothwell pointedly. 'At this rate I'm gonna end up being the laughing-stock of the Stock Growers' Association.'

Conner looked at him uneasily. His own position wasn't exactly becoming any easier.

'I'm supposed to be the law in these parts, Mr Bothwell, and people are gonna start wondering soon why I am not doing something about what's been happening to Ellen Watson. Joe South was killed at the roadhouse and everyone knows he worked for you. And what's more it was Durbin who killed him, coming to the rescue of the woman.'

'I know,' Bothwell snapped at him. 'Goddamnit, I know!'

'And you can't ignore the fact that Averell was a justice of the peace. If we're not careful they're gonna be sending a US marshal here next, to investigate things.'

'So what are you suggesting, Conner? That I let her keep their homesteads?'

'Well, for the moment, anyway. Let things die down a bit. She's lost everything now anyway and can't carry on for much longer,' Conner replied, though not holding out much hope that Bothwell would take his advice.

And he was right.

'I can't wait any longer. I need that water for my cattle now. And besides, what is there to say she will bow out gracefully? She ain't shown any signs of doing so yet.'

'She's stubborn, I'll grant you that,' Conner agreed with him. 'But without the roadhouse she's ruined. Time will prove that.'

Bothwell thought for a moment. He could not risk losing face over the affair. He knew that. If he was to amount to anything in the county, people had to know that he was not someone to be trifled with, least of all by a woman.

'No,' he suddenly declared. 'She's gotta

die. If I have to pull the trigger myself, she's gotta die.'

'Looks like it's the only way it's gonna happen,' Conner remarked.

'You'd think folks round here would thank me for ridding them of that den of iniquity she and their justice of the peace ran,' Bothwell said bitterly.

'Maybe they would, if they thought that was all you were doing,' Conner let slip before he could stop himself. He knew it was going to enrage Bothwell.

'Well, if you'd done your job as you were supposed to and are paid to do and had arrested them for cattle-rustling, the law could have hanged them by now and the matter would be settled,' Bothwell castigated him.

'There weren't no proof that any of their cattle were yours. And besides, when Averell got made justice of the peace, no one was looking for him to be prosecuted for anything,' Conner reasoned with him.

But he knew he was wasting his time. Big shots like Bothwell only got where they were by being ruthless. They didn't tolerate having their ambitions thwarted.

'Well, don't say I didn't warn you,' Conner

dared to say. 'I gotta go through the motions of investigating what's been going on. But if they send a US marshal, he's gonna do more than just that.'

'Leave me to worry about that, Sheriff. This matter is going to be finished with tomorrow one way or the other. I'll pay the woman a visit myself. Maybe it's what I should have done all along.'

'Durbin'll be there,' Conner informed him.

'That's what I'm counting on,' Bothwell replied conspiratorially. 'It's exactly what I'm counting on.'

Sheriff Conner didn't bother to enquire what he meant. Indeed, he preferred not to know, feeling ignorance by far the safest position to be in. He could then honestly say to the people of Casper and the county that he knew nothing of what Bothwell was up to. Not that many of them would believe him, as he well knew. A fact that he now began to fear.

'All right,' he said to Bothwell, backing down, as he knew he had to.

'Get out, Sheriff!' Bothwell snapped at him, all the frustration and anger at not being able to get his own way in a matter that was vital to the empire-building he was set on welling up inside him. 'And don't show your face here again, unless you've something more constructive to say.'

Conner didn't wait to be told a second time to leave. Nor did he say any more to his rotten paymaster. He simply left, showing to Bothwell that he was indeed the gutless creature that the rancher knew him to be.

If Sheriff Conner had shown himself to be lacking in the qualities that made a man a real man, Ellie Watson began to show that she decidedly was not.

'I think it's time I paid Albert Bothwell a visit,' she announced to Durbin and O'Brien.

'What?' Durbin asked her before O'Brien could.

'Well,' Ellie replied defiantly, 'he's been bringing the fight to me long enough. It's time I took it to him, don't you think?'

Durbin and O'Brien looked at her in startled silence. What on earth made her think she could reason with him after all that had happened? Unless, of course, she meant to sell. Both men were thinking the same thoughts but neither wanted to voice them.

Reading them, Ellie said, 'Don't worry, I

am not intending to sell. I just want to ram home the fact.'

'What makes you think he'll listen?' O'Brien asked.

'I'm not talking about talking. I'm talking about doing something,' was Ellie's reply.

She knew exactly what it was she was going to do but it took some persuading to get Durbin and O'Brien to go along with the idea. In the end they only went because she threatened to go without them.

The next day as Bothwell called for his mount to be saddled up and brought round in readiness to depart for Ellie Watson's homestead, she was getting ready to ride to his ranch. Getting ready consisted mainly in donning men's clothing, the trousers of which O'Brien lent her and the shirt of which Durbin did. She'd never worn anything other than dresses and skirts before but figured wearing man's clothing would be more practical for the job she intended to do. And this was no bit of pantomime dressing-up. She was in deadly earnest about what she intended to do and knew her dress had to be practical. Her heart was still breaking but she was angry now too and that anger had to be vented.

Neither she nor Durbin and O'Brien said much to one another as they went about their preparations. Jerry Wheeler and the rest of the workers were going with them and they all had to make sure they were well-armed, as well as making sure they had enough oil-soaked torches to go round. Durbin particularly was still not happy about what Ellie was intending to do but reckoned that with a bit of luck and the element of surprise on their side they might just be OK.

'You ready, boys?' Ellie Watson asked at last.

It was about eleven in the morning and they'd all had a good breakfast. They were living in tents as plans were made for the rebuilding of the roadhouse. As they all indicated that they were ready, Ellie gave the order for them to mount and a few minutes later they were all kicking their horses and following her across the range in the direction of the Round Circle ranch.

TWELVE

At about the same time Bothwell and his men were riding for the roadhouse. Their paths might have crossed had not Durbin decided they'd do best to keep as wide a berth as possible of the Bothwell spread to avoid being spotted by any of his cowboys going about their business of looking after his vast herd of grazing cattle. They were bound to be fewer in number than Bothwell's men and could only lose in a shootout.

Durbin's view of Bothwell remained that of a man formidable in resolve and rich in resources: a man who could never be thwarted. This was not the man who rode on to Ellie Watson's homestead. He did indeed survey a world, small as it was, in ruin. A ruin that he had brought about. But what he knew was that the spirit that had pervaded that world was still very much alive. And he cursed when he found nobody there. In temper he ordered the tents that had been erected to serve as temporary housing to be pulled down and set on fire. There was not much in the tents, all of what Ellie had owned having already been destroyed in the fire that had consumed the roadhouse and its outbuildings. Bothwell, though, took spiteful satisfaction from seeing what there was go up in smoke.

Then he turned his attentions to the livestock.

'Go see if any of them have got anything that looks like our brand on them,' he ordered Jack Green, who had at last got his way in wanting to do his master's dirty work.

Of the few hundred critters that were corralled in Ellie Watson's pens there was none that could truthfully have been identified as rustled cattle stolen from Bothwell's or anyone else's herds. But Jack Green in his hunger to please and gain preference from his boss, declared that there was.

'Right!' snapped an incensed Bothwell.

'Slaughter them all and then set them on fire.'

Jack Green and Bothwell's men didn't have to wait to be told a second time. They had ridden to the roadhouse keyed-up for action and were disappointed to arrive and find there was not going to be any. But now suddenly they'd been given the chance to create the sadistic delight that the unleashing of a thunderously destructive force upon innocents brought to hired hands turned hired thugs. As Ellie Watson's cattle began to trumpet in panic and to fall fatally wounded the air filled with the whoops and hollers of Bothwell's men.

He himself knew that what he'd ordered to be done was futile and wasteful, that he should simply have taken back the cattle. But his aim was to break Ellie Watson's will. The more destruction of her property she saw the sooner that would happen. What he didn't know though was that, far from being near-broken, that will was now being used by her to do more than just survive the worst that he could throw at her; it had been turned into a weapon that had him firmly in its sights. For as he breathed in the smell of cordite and blood,

Ellie Watson and her men were feeling their nostrils fill with the smoke of ranch-house timber.

None of the men and cowboys left at the Round Circle ranch had seen them coming. They had stopped half a mile away to light their torches and then they had spurred their horses into a gallop and didn't stop until they were throwing them through the windows of Bothwell's large and ample ranch house and on to the roof. The place was on fire before anyone realized what was happening.

As some of Bothwell's men came running they recognized Durbin and it soon became apparent to them what was afoot. They watched in horror as O'Brien and Jerry Wheeler threw more flaming torches into the main barn, which was full of hay, and it too began to burn.

It wasn't long before bullets began to fly. Ellie Watson had been persuaded by Durbin and O'Brien that at the moment when that began to happen they would ride. But, now, in the thick of it all and with her adrenalin pumping, she wanted to see Bothwell and to see the look on his face as he witnessed the havoc being wreaked on his own world.

'Come on, Ellie,' Durbin said to her, trying to keep his horse reined in as bullets flew all around them and he fired at Bothwell's men.

'Where is he?' Ellie shouted in reply.

'Hiding or not here,' was Durbin's reply. 'What does it matter, though? We've done what we came here to do. Now let's get out of here before one or all us of get killed.'

As he said it a bullet slammed into Ellie's dappled grey mount's neck. Letting out an agonized whinny it began to collapse under her.

'God!' exclaimed Durbin, turning and firing in all directions at the small but growing number of Round Circle men who were now firing at them.

O'Brien and the others had seen Ellie's horse fall under her and instinctively they spurred or kicked their horses to get close to her. As they formed a protective barrier around her, Ellie, who jumped clear as her horse fell from under her, got to her feet. As she began to collect herself, Durbin rode to her side.

'Come on,' he shouted, offering her a helping hand. 'Get up behind me.'

She did not have to wait to be told a

second time. Grabbing Durbin's hand, she quickly swung up behind him. She had strapped on a Colt .45 before leaving her homestead and had luckily not lost it in the fall.

'Let's get out of here,' Durbin shouted to everyone.

A number of Bothwell's men had fallen, wounded or killed, and Ellie, firing behind her as they rode off, added another one to the list. Miraculously none of her men was even wounded in the shoot-out. Ellie couldn't help but thank God for his mercies, as she and they rode hell for leather away from the Round Circle ranch. She couldn't help but feel, though, that it would have been nice if she had been given the chance to have also taken on Bothwell himself.

THIRTEEN

When Ellie got back to see what Bothwell had done to her tents and livestock she was angry, but what she felt was as nothing compared to the outrage and indignation felt by him on his return to the Round Circle.

'Who the hell does that woman think she is?' he raged, as he stood surveying the burned-out wreck of his ranch house. 'If she thinks she can get away with this, she is wrong. Sorely wrong.'

He didn't know, though, what more he could do to her. He'd destroyed the only property she possessed and had killed all her livestock. What else could he do? Kill her, of course, came the rapid-fire answer. But he knew that by now everyone would know what had happened, both to her and to him, and he realized the whole affair was now being conducted too much in the public glare. This being the case, he decided he was going to make Sheriff Conner earn his money. He was going to have to ensure that she ceased to be a thorn in his side, or else.

'Green,' he said between gritted teeth. 'Go to town and bring Conner here now. And I mean now. And remember,' he said almost as an afterthought, 'we had nothing to do with anything that's happened at the roadhouse. Pretend not to know anything about it at all. Have you got that?'

'Don't worry,' Green replied. 'I ain't no fool, boss.'

Sheriff Conner had indeed heard about what had happened out at the Round Circle ranch but he had barely had time to digest the facts before Jack Green came striding into his office.

'Sheriff,' Green said to Conner by way of a greeting, taking off his Stetson as he stepped into his office.

'Is it true?' were Conner's first words.

'It is,' replied Green, his tone of voice full of incredulity.

'God,' Conner sighed, as he sank back into

his office chair. 'You gotta give it to that woman.'

'Bothwell wants to see you,' Green informed him. 'He said you gotta come now.'

'What about what happened at her place?' Conner asked.

'Don't know nothing about that,' was Green's reply. 'Why, what has happened?'

Sheriff Conner studied him for a moment, knowing that he knew full well what he was talking about. There was no one else in the world who would have done the damage that was done to the tents and livestock at the roadhouse but Bothwell, and Conner grew impatient with the idea that Green or Bothwell might think he wouldn't work on that assumption.

'Don't give me that,' he said to Green tartly. 'You know full well what I am talking about.'

'I told you I don't know nothing. You coming back with me to the Round Circle or what?'

Conner knew he'd be wasting his time, not to mention risking his livelihood, and probably his life, by standing up to Bothwell. But as always he felt that at the very least he had to be seen to be acting impartially.

'Tell him I'll be over later,' he said.

'You best be,' remarked Green, who fancied he had at last stepped into Joe South's and Henry Durbin's shoes and had become Bothwell's main man.

'Yeah,' was all Conner said in reply.

Word of what had happened at the Round Circle ranch soon reached the ears of the other members of the Wyoming Stock Growers' Association and they didn't like it. Things were out of hand and it was beginning to reflect badly on the Association. And no one wanted a US marshal sent to investigate the affair. The biggest shot in the Association was a man called Robert M. Galbraith. He owned a huge ranch running into thousands of acres and had political ambitions. Not wanting any scandal to ruin his chances, he summoned a meeting of the Association, which took place two days after Ellie Watson had set fire to Bothwell's ranch. The meeting took place at his spread, the T bar T ranch.

'Right,' he declared to Bothwell, as the meeting started, 'you'd better tell us what's been going down here.'

Outsiders were never allowed to attend

the Association meetings, which were held in the strictest privacy. This meant everyone could speak frankly and openly.

'I think you all know what's been happening. That goddamn woman refuses to sell and now she's burnt down my ranch house,' Bothwell declared in exasperated tones.

'How d'you let that happen?' asked another of the members, Tom Sun.

'I didn't,' was Bothwell's reply. 'I wasn't there. But anyway would any one of you expect someone to ride on to your ranch in broad daylight and burn down your damned ranch house. It just don't happen.'

'Look, Albie,' Galbraith said. 'We can all sympathize with your predicament, but you've gotta do something about this woman. You've let things get out of hand and it doesn't reflect very well on the Association.'

'After all,' added Sun, 'you dealt effectively enough with her partner, Jim Averell. Why haven't you dealt with her?'

That a woman was getting the better of him had made Bothwell feel humiliated and he felt that humiliation all the more now in front of his peers.

'It's because she is a woman that my men

have found it hard to do what they should have,' he replied, feeling hot under the collar and pulling it down with a finger to let in some air. 'And one of them's even gone over to her side.'

'But the woman's a whore,' remarked another of the members. 'Everyone knows it. I can't imagine anyone would complain if you were to rid the county of her like. Indeed, I should think it would be deemed a public service.'

The other members voiced their agreement.

'Well, it appears, gentlemen,' Galbraith declared, 'that this is a pressing matter that really does need to be taken in hand. The whore is clearly out of control and needs to be dealt with. Do you think, Albert, that you are up to it or do you need help?'

This was too much for Bothwell, who felt he had been humiliated enough, without someone else being called in to do his dirty work for him, especially where a female was concerned.

'Of course I can handle it myself,' he replied in snappy tones.

'Well, just make sure you do,' Galbraith said. 'Before any more harm is done.'

That more or less brought the meeting to a close and as Bothwell left he recalled the meeting he'd had with Sheriff Conner after he'd sent for him. There were witnesses enough, he'd told him, to prosecute the woman for what she'd done and he'd told him to get out there and arrest her. He had also told him that no one would shed any tears if she were to be shot while trying to resist arrest. Conner hadn't liked it but Bothwell had put him straight over that, pointing out to him that it was now his neck or hers that was on the line. It seemed to have some impact upon him and Bothwell could only hope that Conner would do what he was told. Conner had worried some in regard to what folk were saying about what had happened out at the roadhouse, but there were no witnesses, only speculation, and everyone had to admit you couldn't go to law with just that.

As Bothwell rode away from the T bar T ranch he decided that he'd have to send Jack Green into town to see what, if anything, Conner had achieved. If the answer was nothing, then the matter would have to be dealt with some other way. And Conner? Well, he'd be dealt with too.

FOURTEEN

Sheriff Conner couldn't find Ellie Watson. He'd ridden out to the roadhouse but there was no sign of her there. There were the burned-out remnants of the tents and the partially burned carcasses of her cattle but no sign of Ellie. He rode back to town to be confronted by Jack Green.

'There ain't no sign of her nor anyone at the roadhouse,' Conner told him.

'Well, you'd better find her. It ain't just Bothwell who wants her now. It's the whole Association. They think things is out of hand and they want her strung up.'

Green was one of those creepy sort of characters who thinks he's something more than he is.

'I'll find her,' an irritated Sheriff Conner told him impatiently. 'But if she ain't nowhere to be found, maybe it's because she's finally got the message and cleared out.'

'It'll be best for her, if she has,' Green remarked.

Inwardly Conner laughed to himself at how inconsequential any views Green might have on the matter were, but outwardly he showed no signs of it. You didn't mess with the likes of Bothwell, let alone the Association, and he didn't want Green going and giving Bothwell the wrong impression about how hard he was trying to find Ellie Watson and arrest her.

'Go back to Bothwell and tell him I'm putting together a posse to hunt for her. If she's still in the county, we'll find her. Just tell him that,' he said to him.

'You best make sure you do find her,' were Green's parting words.

Conner threw him a contemptuous look as he left his office. He had two deputies but apart from them he didn't know whose interest he could rouse enough to make up a posse to go hunt down a woman most people admired for standing up to a big shot like Bothwell. Casper wasn't the sort of town that attracted the kind of low-life that'd do anything to earn a drinking buck or two. But then he wasn't that serious himoolf about trying to find Ellie Watson. Except that he did value his job and he worried that it was in the power of the Association to take it away from him.

Ellie Watson, along with O'Brien, Durbin and the rest, was hiding out at Horse Creek, north of Bothwell's spread. She wasn't too concerned about the loss of her livestock, because she had an idea about how she could replace them. Both Durbin and O'Brien had tried to talk her out of it but without any success. She had the bit between her teeth now and wasn't going to let it go easily.

'You know how they work, Henry,' Ellie said to Durbin. 'When's the best time to do it?'

'Night-time is always the best. That's when there's the least number of cowboys watching over the dogies and it's easiest to cut 'em out without being seen,' was Durbin's reply. 'But are you really sure about this, Ellie?'

'It's the last thing Bothwell'll be expecting us to do.'

'Yeah, but he'll come and take them straight back.'

'He'll have to find them and us first,' Ellie replied.

'And he will.'

'Well, then we'll give him a fight.'

Durbin wasn't happy with Ellie's reply but then he didn't really know what sort of reply he would have been happy with. Ellie could see this.

'Look, Henry,' she said. 'All I really want to do is wreak havoc with Bothwell's outfit. He killed Jim and burnt down the road-house. He can't just be allowed to get away with it. He ain't nothing but a man—'

'Yeah, and a mighty powerful one, in these parts anyway,' O'Brien interrupted.

'Only if he's allowed to be,' replied Ellie. 'Besides, what have we got to lose. He's ruined me. There ain't much else he can do to me.'

'Except kill ya, or get the law to do it,' suggested Durbin.

'Like he did Jim and Josh,' interjected O'Brien.

'That makes it nice and simple then, don't it?'

O'Brien, Durbin and the rest could only

stand in awe of her. They knew she meant it. And knowing so, they felt they wanted to be there at her side. Otherwise, what sort of men could they call themselves?

'All right,' Durbin said. 'Whatever you say, Ellie.'

'Good,' was Ellie's reply. 'We'll do it tonight.'

'What does he mean he can't find her?' Bothwell railed at Jack Green.

'She ain't at the roadhouse. There ain't no one there. He said he was gonna get together a posse and go hunt for her,' Green informed his boss, feeling important for being the messenger.

'Where does he think she is?' Bothwell asked.

He wasn't really expecting Green to give him an answer. He was instead merely thinking out loud.

'Maybe she's cleared out. Maybe she finally got the message and has cleared out,' he thought out loud.

'That's what Conner said,' Green informed him.

Bothwell had set up home in one of the bunkhouses. Work had already begun on rebuilding the farmhouse but it was going to be a while before it was ready to live in again. No matter how long it took to rebuild it, he knew he had the money to do it; Ellie Watson would not have the money to rebuild the roadhouse. And he could make sure no one gave her the credit facilities to do it. Not the bank, which was owned by Association members, nor the general store in town, which Association members also owned. She'd know this. But, then, why didn't she take the money that was on offer for her and Averell's homesteads? If she had decided to clear out of the county she'd need something to start up again somewhere else. And what about Durbin? If he was behind her, as he knew he was, he wouldn't let her walk away empty handed. Except, of course, that it was he who had put the noose around her lover's neck. Maybe it was he who was encouraging her to get out of the county before she found out. Maybe, just maybe, then, he had won the game after all. Yeah, maybe that was it. Maybe he had.

So his thoughts were running, but they were not thoughts he shared with Jack Green.

'All right,' he said to him. 'Maybe Conner's

right. Time will tell. We can wait.'

'But what about Durbin?' Green asked.

'What about him?'

'You gonna let him get away with what he's done?'

'Well, who's gonna go after him and punish him? You?' Bothwell asked, mockingly.

Green was sporting a Colt .45 but he'd never fired it in anger. His right hand went down to it now and rested upon its handle.

'If you were to order me to, I would,' was his disconsolate reply. 'There ain't no one else.'

'Which is why we're gonna wait and see if Conner finds them or not.'

Bothwell didn't have anything else to say to Green and Green knew it. Maybe, he thought, as he left, he should go out and look for them himself. That would show Bothwell. And if he brought back the woman and Durbin, dead or alive, that would show him, too. But it was nearly sunup. Maybe he best sleep on it. And then if he decided to do it, he could do it the next day.

Bothwell was left alone with his thoughts. As he looked about him at his surroundings his anger and indignation knew no bounds.

He was going to spend the night in a bunk. Thinking of the woman who had reduced him to such straits, he just hoped for her sake that she had indeed fled the county. Because, if she hadn't, and Conner found her, she'd swing. He had the power to make sure she did and he'd use it.

FIFTEEN

It was obvious that a storm was blowing up. A meteorological storm, that is. There was a slight chill in the air coupled with a strange kind of electrical charge that made all living creatures feel restless. Among them was Ellie Watson and her men.

'What do you think?' Ellie asked Durbin, looking up at the night sky, which despite the darkness could be seen to be obviously cloud-laden.

'It might help us. It might hinder us. Depends how you look upon it,' replied Durbin.

'How d'you mean?'

'Well, most people out in it are gonna be concentrating on surviving it and those who don't absolutely need to be out in it are gonna stay in.'

'Trouble is,' interjected O'Brien, 'we ain't got any slickers to keep the rain off and without one you can get fairly swamped.'

Ellie heard what both men were saying and thought about what would be best. She knew if they were going to do anything it had to be done soon. She couldn't believe that either Bothwell or Sheriff Conner, either separately or, as was more likely, combined, would leave them at liberty for long.

'I don't reckon as we've got much choice when it comes to it. It feels to me like it's now or never. I suppose we've become outlaws and are soon gonna be hunted down,' she declared.

Hearing what she said made Durbin feel uncomfortable. Ellie Watson was no kind of outlaw, at least not in the accepted sense of the word. She was no Jesse James or Billy the Kid. She'd simply fought back in self-defence and any honest court in Wyoming Territory would see that. Except he knew that she wouldn't be coming up before an honest court. At least not in Sweetwater County.

They were going to cut out from Bothwell's herd about two hundred cattle to compensate Ellie for those he'd slaughtered at the roadhouse. But what then? he asked her.

'I ain't thought that far,' replied Ellie.

In reality, of course, she'd thought things through but only in so far as she had decided to take the rustled cattle back to the homestead and await developments.

'Well, what are we gonna do with Bothwell's cattle once we've taken them?' O'Brien asked.

'Take them to the roadhouse and see what happens,' Ellie replied.

'And if Bothwell comes to try and take 'em back?'

'He'll have a fight on his hands, then, won't he? In fact I rather relish the thought of that.'

'Ain't you afraid of dying?' Jerry Wheeler asked her.

'Of course I am, Jerry. But what have I got to live for, if I let Bothwell win? He's already killed Jim.'

The mention of Jim's death made Durbin

squirm. He couldn't help but wonder when Ellie was going to find out that it had been he who had led the gang that strung him up. Perhaps they'd both die before she found out. He could have wished for that, except that he wanted Ellie to get the better of Bothwell. She was the underdog and once he'd realized that this was what she was he hadn't wanted her to be beaten. And anyway, why should she die just to save his own guilty face?

'Well,' he declared, wanting to cut talk of Jim's death short, 'let's do it, then. Let's ride. By the time we get to Bothwell's spread the hour will be about right.'

As they rode away from what had been their temporary camp, a few spots of rain began to fall. By the time they arrived at their destination the wind was up and it was pouring steadily. In the distance, coming closer, judging by how long it took the thunder to follow, lightning began to flash. Durbin was an experienced cowboy and O'Brien and Wheeler had some experience. As they came upon the herd the latter two took Durbin's instructions.

'And remember,' he said to Ellie, raising his voice to be heard above the growing storm, 'if the herd stampedes, get ahead of it. Don't try to ride against it.' Then, for the benefit of everyone, he added, 'And no one's to shoot unless shot at.'

Arriving on Bothwell's spread, they had looked around for nightriders but had not seen any. Durbin knew there had to be some. The herd was large, though, and spread wide over Bothwell's land. But they were on the edge of it and he reckoned if they were lucky they might be able to cut out the few hundred cattle they intended to rustle without being noticed. He knew they'd be lucky if this did turn out to be the case, but it wasn't impossible given the weather.

The weather was turning wild, making the cattle frightened and restless. When an animal as dumb as a cow feels fear its instincts are to try and run away, imagining it can leave the threat behind. Amongst a herd of cattle this is when a stampede can happen. Most of the time it doesn't though. Cattle know about storms and before they become entirely spooked the storm passes and the herd soon settles down again. But only if an extra dimension is not introduced into the affair. The shock of gunfire can be that extra dimension. Thunder has a natural sound to it; gunfire does not. It's metallic and sharp and feels directed. Bursting in on the eardrums of any living creature, it pushes it over the edge.

But so far, so good. There had not been any gunfire yet and Durbin and his men were managing to separate a number of cattle from the main herd. And then in the blinding flash of a fork of lightning right above their heads they were seen by one of the Round Circle's nightriders. The collar of his slicker was pulled up around his neck and his Stetson was pulled down about his face and head. Nevertheless the lightning flash had so illuminated the area around him that he couldn't fail to see what he had least expected to see, other human beings in number, if only small. He knew instantly what they must be up to. And he knew, too, the dangers of challenging them in such unhelpful weather. But he couldn't just let them get away with what they were obviously up to.

'Hey!' he called out to Durbin, who was nearest, as a burst of thunder began to roll near them.

Durbin didn't hear him.

'Hey!' the nightrider called out again, this time spurring his horse to ride in the direction of Durbin. As he rode he drew his rifle, a Winchester, and pulled down the trigger guard to put a bullet into the chamber.

Just then there was another flash of lightning and as it lit up the skies Durbin caught a glimpse of the nightrider coming towards him.

'What are you doing?' the nightrider called out to him.

But it wasn't a question the nightrider expected an answer to. It was more just thinking out loud. Both he and Durbin knew that any sudden disturbance could cause the herd to stampede. Equally both men knew the other would have him in his sights, either to force him to surrender or to fire his weapon.

Durbin drew his own rifle. The night was dark again and he couldn't see the nightrider but he knew he was there. Then as his eyes began to recover their night vision he saw him in outline. Coming up behind him was another figure. It looked like O'Brien. Whoever it was he had in his hand a Winchester, which, it was evident, he was intending to use as a club.

There was suddenly another flash of lightning and Durbin clearly saw O'Brien knock the nightrider from his horse. But then it was dark again and Durbin could see nothing. Kicking his horse he rode to where he knew the nightrider and O'Brien to be. He found both men wrestling with one another in what they were whipping up into a sea of mud. It was making the cattle amongst them want to get away. Durbin was afraid they were going to start a stampede.

'Stop it,' he shouted out to the men. 'Stop it before you make the herd stampede.'

O'Brien and the nightrider were not slow to obey his instructions. In the back of both men's minds as they fought was the fear of being trampled to death under the feet of cattle spooked by their fighting. Added to this, the nightrider recognized Durbin's voice.

'Is that you, Durbin?' he asked, peering at him through the pouring rain and the wind that was driving it.

Durbin in turn recognized the rider. He was an experienced old hand called Orrin Fleming. He'd never got involved in

Bothwell's heavy-handed tactics but he and Durbin had respected one another for being good at their cowboy jobs. Still, Durbin knew he had to keep the advantage.

'What if it is?' he asked him.

'Well, what are you playing at?' Orrin Fleming asked him.

'Never mind that,' was Durbin's reply. 'You gonna let me get on with it or am I gonna have to kill you?'

Fleming knew that Durbin was serious. He knew too that he was outnumbered.

'Well, I guess you've got your reasons for doing what you're doing and if you take my guns away there ain't much I can do to stop you now, is there?' was his shrewd reply.

'Or you could join us,' Durbin suggested to him. 'I'm with Ellie Watson.'

'Now you know, Henry, I don't get involved in anyone's fights. Just finish what you've started and I won't try to stop you.'

'Take his guns,' Durbin instructed O'Brien, who by now had collected himself, even though he was soaked to the core and muddier than a pig in its sty.

'Are there any more of you?' Durbin asked Fleming.

'Not close by,' Fleming replied, straightening his slicker and looking around for his horse, which was near by.

'I've got your word, Orrin, have I?' Durbin asked, clearly meaning that Fleming had said he wouldn't interfere.

'I gave it, didn't I?' was all Fleming replied, as he swung up on to his mount.

He then turned his horse and rode off into the darkness. Durbin watched him go for a second or two and then turned to O'Brien and said:

'Come on. Let's get this finished.'

Neither Ellie nor the others were aware of what had happened. The storm was beginning to pass and they'd cut out from the herd as many cattle as they intended to take in recompense for what Bothwell had done. The problem now was to keep them together and drive them in the dark to the roadhouse homestead. But they all knew the lie of the land and, as the rain slackened off, were confident they could do it.

'You reckon he'll keep to his word?' O'Brien asked, riding up close to Durbin and obviously referring to Fleming, whose name he hadn't known.

'It's a chance we'll have to take,' was Durbin's reply.

But he knew Fleming well and had no fears.

SIXTEEN

'What's that smoke?' one of Sheriff Conner's deputies asked him.

Conner had managed to get together enough men to form a posse, small though it was, and the morning after the storm he had led them out to scour the range in search of Ellie Watson and her men.

Bringing the posse from a steady trot to a halt, Conner replied, 'Yeah, what is it? Looks like it's coming from the roadhouse. But no one's there.'

Conner thought for a moment, raising himself up in his saddle and looking around. It was definitely Ellie Watson's place, but he couldn't see what was left there to burn and produce so much smoke.

He decided he had better go and investigate.

'We'd better go and take a look,' he said to his deputy, kicking his horse into a gallop.

By the time they arrived at the roadhouse the fire that had produced the smoke Conner's deputy had spotted had become an inferno. It was the pile of bloated and rotting cattle killed by Bothwell. Conner could not believe his eyes, not so much at the sight of the fire, but at the large herd of cattle collected in the cattle pen. Ellie Watson was not afraid of Conner. She was contemptuous of him, and the law in the county, but she was not afraid. So she let him ride unchallenged on to her homestead.

'What's going on, Ellie?' he asked, looking around him to indicate he meant the fire and the herd of cattle.

'What do you think, Sheriff? We're doing some clearing up and making room for my new stock,' was Ellie's reply.

Durbin and O'Brien, who were busy managing the carcasses' fire, hadn't at first seen Conner and his men ride up, but once they had they left what they were doing and hurried to Ellie's side. First, though, they strapped on their gun belts, which had been thrown over the top rail of the cattle pen. They were just in time to hear Sheriff Conner ask Ellie where she'd got the new stock from.

Ellie saw no need to lie. She was out to confront Bothwell's power in the county, not to hide from it.

'Took it from the man who slaughtered mine,' she said defiantly.

Standing either side of her, Durbin and O'Brien braced themselves for Conner's response.

'You what?' Conner asked incredulously.

'I said we took 'em from Bothwell. Reckoned he owed them to me. Why, has he sent you here to take them back?'

'No, no,' Conner replied, nonplussed and confused by what he had heard. 'And he let you?' he asked.

'Of course not,' interjected Durbin. 'He may not even know yet we've got them. We took them last night under cover of the storm.'

'You know that's a hanging offence, don't you?' Conner declared, looking at Ellie. 'You just played straight into Bothwell's hands.'

'You know what he did to my stock. Ain't that just as criminal an offence?' Ellie asked.

'Who said it was Bothwell that did it? There ain't no witnesses to the fact, whereas everyone on the ranch saw you and Durbin and the rest here burn down his ranch house. I'm gonna have to take you and them in, Ellie. You ain't left me with any choice.'

As he said the words "take you in" Durbin, followed closely by O'Brien, drew his gun. Following suit behind Conner and his posse, were Wheeler and the others of Ellie's men. A chorus of clicks was heard as they all cocked their triggers.

Conner and his posse of men looked around them, stirring nervously in their saddles as they realized they were surrounded.

'What the. . . ?' Conner began.

'We ain't going nowhere, Conner. You've known all along that Bothwell's been harassing us for our land and that he had Jim killed and you ain't done nothing about it. You ain't the law around here, Bothwell is. So if he wants me and my men arrested, tell him to come and do it himself. Otherwise we ain't going nowhere.'

Conner looked from Ellie to Durbin. If he deserved damning, didn't Durbin deserve it, too? But what he didn't know was whether Ellie knew about the leading part Durbin had played in the killing of Jim Averell. He looked straight into Durbin's eyes, giving him a look that he hoped warned him he was, by taking sides with Ellie, walking on very dangerous ground.

Durbin was no fool and easily read Conner's look. He decided that if Conner divulged anything to Ellie he'd first deny it and then, if necessary, he'd shut him up with a bullet.

But Conner said nothing about it. The game wasn't up yet and he had his own back to watch.

'All right,' he said instead to Ellie. 'But you can be sure he will come and it'll be no good then asking me for protection.'

'Ha!' Ellie laughed scornfully out loud. 'As if you've given any to date.'

But Conner ignored her.

'Come on, men,' he said to his posse, reining his horse around, 'let's go.' Then adding for the benefit of Ellie, 'Don't say I didn't warn you.'

Ellie, Durbin and the others watched them go in silence. Then at last O'Brien asked Durbin:

129

'What d'you think?'

'We'd better prepare ourselves,' was all Durbin said in reply.

Someone else who had spotted smoke coming from the roadhouse was Jack Green. Having slept on things the night before, he had decided he would ride out in search of Ellie Watson and Durbin. He had come close enough to the homestead to witness the confrontation between them and Sheriff Conner and then stopped and taken cover. It looked to him as it was and he knew his boss would be very interested to hear about it. And the cattle? Where had they come from? He decided he had to ride back to the Round Circle and put the question to Bothwell.

SEVENTEEN

Bothwell sent for his foreman and it was soon ascertained exactly where Ellie Watson's new cattle had come from.

'Right!' declared Bothwell, 'We ride in the morning. I want every available hand to ride with me. If it means I take fifty men, then I take them. Have you got that?'

The foreman had indeed got the message. If the war against Ellie Watson was going to be won, it meant the deployment of the whole army and all its resources. Yes, he had got the message OK. And soon the message would be relayed to the other members of the Wyoming Cattle Growers' Association and they were not happy about it. This was taking a sledgehammer to crack a nut and it was reflecting badly upon them. Robert M. Galbraith, their chairman, decided to send for Bothwell and Sheriff Conner.

'I thought you were going to bring an end to this matter,' he said to Bothwell when both men were present in his office.

He and Conner had received their summonses to appear before the Association forthwith and both knew that this had meant now, immediately.

'Which is what I am doing and it will end tomorrow,' Bothwell declared.

Galbraith, unconvinced, turned his attentions to Sheriff Conner.

'Henry,' he said. 'And what are you doing about this woman?'

'Well, it's difficult, Bob,' Conner answered. 'The whole town, let alone the county, has got its eyes focused on this affair and at the moment everyone's laying all their ills squarely at Albert here's feet. And we mustn't forget that Jim Averell was a justice of the peace and a popular one at that.'

'Albert?' Galbraith said, inviting Bothwell to have his say.

'I had to have that land, Bob, and you know that. I didn't know my men were gonna turn all lily-livered on me, but I have taken control of the situation now and by tomorrow that woman will be reunited with her husband.'

Sheriff Conner looked uneasy at what Bothwell had said.

'Don't you think it might be better if things were left alone for a while, Albert, just until interest in the affair dies down some,' he suggested.

'That woman stole two hundred head of my cattle the other night. Do you think she should be allowed to get away with that?' Bothwell asked in exasperated tones.

'Yeah, but you slaughtered all of hers,' Conner replied.

'Whose side are you on, Henry?' Bothwell asked pointedly.

'You know the answer to that.'

'Well, it doesn't look like it to me. If you'd arrested that woman this morning, she could be swinging this time next week and the whole goddamn business would be over.'

'What makes you think a jury would convict her, after all that's gone on?' Conner threw back at him, 'Especially when they send a US marshal down to investigate things.'

'Gentlemen, gentlemen, please.' Galbraith interrupted them.

'Well,' Bothwell sneered, 'what the hell do we pay this man for?'

'Not to openly turn a blind eye to murder. You're supposed to be more discreet than that,' Conner said.

'This is getting us nowhere,' Galbraith declared. 'We're gonna have to approach this matter from another angle. I've been giving it some thought and I've come to the conclusion a little mediation is called for. At least, what is seen to be mediation. We will send someone to talk to the woman. They'll try and persuade her to give you back your cattle and to go to litigation over the slaughter of her own. We'll pretend we don't know who's behind her troubles but that we're going to investigate. In the meantime, until the outcome of those investigations is known, a truce is to be declared between you. Then three months down the line you can kill her, Albert, only this time try to do it quickly and cleanly.'

Bothwell did not find the prospect of waiting three months to remove the thorn from his side very appealing but at the same time he knew that he probably had no choice. You did not argue with the Association once it had made a pronouncement on a matter and he knew that Galbraith spoke with the voice of the Association.

'She burnt down my ranch house,' he commented to Galbraith.

'And she'll pay for it,' Galbraith declared.

And Durbin? Bothwell asked himself.

The answer, which remained unspoken, was that he'd die, too. Maybe sooner: in town, on the range, somewhere. Anywhere.

'I've been humiliated,' he remarked out loud.

'Revenge,' suggested Galbraith, 'is a dish best taken cold.'

'And you haven't helped,' Bothwell said, turning to Conner. 'Maybe it's time we elected a new sheriff.'

Conner was about to reply when he was stopped by Galbraith saying, 'Let's just say the whole thing could and should have been handled differently. Meanwhile, if we limit the damage already done in the way I have suggested this affair can still turn out satisfactorily for all concerned.'

Bothwell and Conner were both aware of Galbraith's political ambitions and they could both see that what he was suggesting now was a political solution. For his part, Bothwell could see Galbraith was a man he might want as a friend in the future and for this reason he realized he had to acquiesce in what he was asking him to do. Sheriff Conner, on the other hand, simply knew that his survival depended on doing what his paymasters, the Wyoming Stock Growers' Association, ordered him to do.

'All right,' Bothwell agreed. 'Three months.'

'Anything that enables me to be seen to be doing my job,' Sheriff Conner said in compliance.

'All right,' said Galbraith, satisfied.

Then he went on to detail exactly what was to happen next. The following day a delegation of Association members, along with Conner and his deputies, was to go to the Watson homestead and put to Ellie Watson what had been decided upon. She was to be persuaded it was in her best interests to go along with it. Everyone was to be seen to be following things through, the law in particular, and then . . . well, then the matter would be brought to a satisfactory end and everyone would be happy.

Galbraith, who could see that Bothwell was not happy with the solution to the problem but that he saw the sense of it, made sure he understood things by saying, 'Albert?'

'OK,' Bothwell replied, though his mind was patently elsewhere, perhaps coming up with other solutions.

'Good!' Galbraith declared, adding, 'The delegation will arrive at your offices at nine in the morning, Hal.'

With that the matter was closed and Bothwell and Conner departed, to go their separate ways. Bothwell, though, was not a happy man. He didn't think he could wait three months and didn't altogether see why he should. He had been humiliated enough. The whole county had witnessed it but there was going to be no more of it.

EIGHTEEN

On the ride back to his Round Circle ranch Bothwell decided that if the Association's delegation was to be at Conner's office at nine the next morning, he'd be at the roadhouse by eight. Surprise, he reckoned, giving him the advantage it had given Ellie Watson when she had attacked the Round Circle. By the time the delegation and Conner and his deputies arrived there it'd all be over and they'd find their services were no longer required. That only those of the town's undertaker were.

He left the Round Circle with fifty or so men. Orrin Flemmg was not one of them, but Green was at their head after

Bothwell. There was going to be a blood-
bath and, he hoped, the chance for
Bothwell to see how invaluable his
services to him really were.

Bothwell might have achieved his tacti-
cal advantage had not a young cowboy
seen him and his men as they rode to the
roadhouse homestead. It was the same
young cowboy who had come to Ellie's aid
the time Durbin had come to see her at
the roadhouse. He had been on his way to
Spring Rock to see his family and hoping
to become engaged to a childhood sweet-
heart. He was now on his way back to the
T bar T ranch, Galbraith's spread, where
he worked. He somehow guessed what
Bothwell and his men were up to and
decided to ride hell for leather to warn
Ellie Watson. He was heading there
anyway, having no idea the ranchhouse
had been burned down.

Keeping less than ten minutes ahead of
Bothwell, he arrived just as the tented
roadhouse was beginning to surface. Jerry
Wheeler had been on night watch and he
saw the young cowboy riding full pelt for
the homestead. Wheeler had a Henry .44
rifle and would have taken a shot at

Owen, had he not so obviously been a lone rider. Added to which something told him that a man riding at such a speed so purposefully was more likely to be a messenger than an attacker. So he ran to Durbin's tent to tell him of his imminent arrival. By the time Durbin had registered what he was being told the young cowboy was only 500 yards away. He had just managed to strap on his gun and holster by the time the young man arrived.

'Men,' gasped the young rider, as he brought his horse to a halt. 'Must be at least a half a hundred of them riding fast for here. They can only be a few minutes away.'

He and Durbin recognized one another straight away.

'It's all right,' Ellie, who came out of her tent, which was next to Durbin's, at the same time as the young cowboy arrived, informed him. 'He's on our side now.'

The young cowboy was pleased to hear it. The sight of the burned-out ruin of the roadhouse had made him suddenly fearful that Ellie's fight with Bothwell, of which, like all the county, he knew, had already been lost. But before he could even greet Ellie, Durbin had sprung into action.

'It's got to be Bothwell,' Durbin announced. 'Pull the wagons together,' he then ordered O'Brien and Wheeler, referring to two wagons standing nearby. 'Here, in front of the tents.'

The four men quickly put the wagons in place and with a supreme effort, aided by Ellie and her other hands, who had all come running, turned them on their sides to provide cover.

'Right,' continued Durbin, 'now, everybody, go get your guns and bring all the ammunition you've got.'

'Shouldn't we send somebody to Casper for Sheriff Conner?' Ellie asked him, as the others ran to their tents.

Durbin thought for a second, wondering if there was any point, and then said, 'Maybe we should all just run, if there's as many of them as he says. What's your name, boy?'

'Tex, sir, Tex Owen,' the young cowboy informed him.

'How many men did you say were coming?'

'A lot. Three, maybe four dozen.'

Durbin threw Ellie a worried look.

'I don't care how many of them there are, I ain't running nowhere,' Ellie said firmly. 'This is my land and I aim to defend it.'

This was the stance Ellie had taken all along and it was what Durbin expected of her now.

'I know that, Ellie,' he said to her, as O'Brien and the others returned with their guns and ammunition, 'but it's more than likely going to be suicide this time.'

'Ain't it always been?' was Ellie's reply.

Durbin didn't argue with her. Perhaps, he couldn't help but think to himself, death was preferable anyway to Ellie finding out that it was he who had put the noose around her lover's neck.

'All right,' he said, turning to the others and looking over the wagons for a sight of Bothwell and his men. 'Open fire as soon as they ride into range.'

'What about sending someone to Casper for the sheriff?' Ellie asked again.

Durbin again thought for a moment. 'All right,' he said, looking at Wheeler, who was the youngest amongst them. 'You go,' he said to him, thinking that if anyone's life was to be saved, it should be his.

But Wheeler wasn't happy about being chosen.

'Wouldn't it be better if you went, Ellie,' he said, looking at Ellie and then Durbin, adding, 'I mean Ellie being a woman and all.'

All the men present, Durbin included, would have agreed with him, had not Ellie been the owner of the land the fight was all about. But more to the point, had she not shown she was every bit as good as any man they'd ever ridden with.

'I'm staying,' was all Ellie said in reply to what Wheeler had suggested. 'Now get, Jerry, and ride like hell. We'll hold out for as long as we can.'

As Jerry ran to saddle up his horse, Bothwell and his men appeared in a cloud of dust in the distance.

'Here they come,' announced O'Brien, who was the first to see them.

'You don't have to stay,' Durbin turned and said to Tex Owen, who'd taken up a place standing behind the wagon with the others.

'Maybe not,' Owen replied, looking about him and then at Ellie, who was still dressed in man's clothes. 'But I ain't leaving either.'

'Good,' was all Durbin said in reply, remembering with some uneasiness the time the young cowboy had faced him down in the roadhouse and forced him to leave. 'Right,' he said to them all, as he took up his own position behind the wagon. 'Don't fire until I give the order to and make every bullet count.'

They all waited and watched tensely as Bothwell and his army of men drew closer. They heard Wheeler start his ride to Casper for the sheriff but none of them harboured any false hopes that he'd be able to get there and bring back help in time.

Ellie began to wonder if she'd done right in asking the young men around her to risk their lives for her. It was too late now though. Her mind filled with a picture of her lover Jim and her heart filled with hatred for the man who had robbed her of him.

'Steady,' she heard Durbin saying.

Focusing the sights of her Winchester rifle on what was obviously the leader of the men riding towards them and who she assumed, though she could not make him out clearly yet, had to be Bothwell, she waited, keen to let her first shot go.

'Steady,' Durbin said again.

Then, when the riders were only a few hundred yards away, he gave the order to fire. Ellie's shot went well wide of its mark, leaving Bothwell still seated on his saddle, though it killed one of his men.

Bothwell hadn't known what he was leading his men into until the last minute. It had been his intention simply to ride on to the homestead with guns blasting, killing anything that moved. Having been greeted with a barrage of gunfire he had suddenly to change his tactics. Six or more of his men had fallen. As more fell, Green amongst them, he turned them around and led them to the safety of a clump of trees nearby.

What now? he couldn't help but ask himself.

Ellie Watson's men kept up their barrage of fire and Bothwell's men returned it, shooting at will. While the wagons they were hiding behind became peppered with bullet holes, neither Ellie nor any of her men were hit. But each side was now pinned down by the other and Bothwell began to realize that this was how the situation could remain until the Association's delegation and Sheriff Conner showed up. He would be forced to back down, which would lead to yet more humiliation. He began to contemplate the idea of simply leading his men in a cavalry-style charge on Ellie Watson and her men. More of his men would die but surely enough of them would get through and be able to overwhelm Ellie Watson's men and kill them all, her included. After a few more minutes' thought, he decided that this was what he would have to do.

NINETEEN

Jerry Wheeler had almost ridden his horse into the ground in his haste to get to Casper. He had no illusions that Sheriff Conner would necessarily act with integrity and rush to Ellie's aid but he hoped that something – anything – would be done to save her and the others.

He in fact never reached Casper. He was a mile or more outside of town when he came across Conner accompanied by the Association's delegation on its way to the roadhouse homestead. They were proceeding at a steady trot down the old Oregon Trail when they saw him coming at speed towards them. Wheeler didn't know who they were at first and thought to ride off the trail and give them a wide berth, fearing they might be more men coming to join in the attack on Ellie. Then he recognized Conner amongst them.

'Where are you going in such a hurry, boy?' Sheriff Conner asked him as he pulled up in front of them.

Fighting to catch his breath, Wheeler replied:

'Ellie Watson is under attack at the road-house and I was sent to get help.'

'Under attack? What do you mean?' Conner asked him, looking from one delegation member to another, fearing he knew from whom Ellie Watson was under attack.

'From Bothwell,' gasped Wheeler, between breaths. 'He arrived with dozens of men and there's only a few to defend Ellie. Something's got to be done or Bothwell will surely kill her.'

Conner turned in his saddle to face Tom Sun, who was head of the Association's delegation.

'What do you think, Tom?' he asked.

Sun didn't answer straight away. Stirring restlessly in his saddle as if trying to find a comfortable seat, he thought about the matter. Inside he was seething to think that Bothwell had deliberately gone against the

Association's will. He had already risked bringing the Association into disrepute and what he was doing now would reflect very badly on its doings. He knew Galbraith would be a very unhappy man once he heard. But the situation need not necessarily be utterly hopeless. There was a way of salvaging something out of it that could be of benefit to the Association.

'You sure it's Bothwell?' he asked Wheeler.

'Couldn't be anyone else, sir,' was Wheeler's reply.

Sun and the others didn't doubt him.

'All right,' Sun said, assuming an air of noble gallantry, 'we'd better hurry to Miss Watson's rescue.'

Bothwell did not easily persuade his men to make a charge on Ellie and her men. Green would have jumped at the opportunity to demonstrate to his boss his unfailing obedience. But he was dead and better men than he were left serving Bothwell.

'Don't you think it's a bit risky, boss?' said one of them, who'd worked for Bothwell a long time, and who was in his mature years. 'Wouldn't it be better just to wait until they run out of ammunition, which they must surely do sooner or later?'

Bothwell knew the man was right, but he had other concerns the man was not aware of.

'Who's boss around here?' he demanded of the cowboy in what to his men was an uncharacteristic manner. They knew he had good cause to hate the woman. She had after all burned down his ranch house and stolen his cattle. But it seemed to them he had lost his head.

'You, Mr Bothwell,' the cowboy said.

'Well, then,' Bothwell snarled. 'Do as I tell you.'

As Bothwell spoke a bullet thumped into the tree behind which he was hiding, causing a shower of splinters to hit him in the face.

'Well?' It caused him to snarl even more angrily at his men. 'You with me or not?'

'We're with you,' replied the cowboy, realizing they had no real choice in the matter.

'Right, then,' Bothwell declared, relieved. 'Let's get to it.'

Once the shoot-out had started, Durbin had begun to feel optimistic that they might be able to hold out until help arrived from

Casper. He wasn't entirely convinced Sheriff Conner could be relied upon to do his job, but he hoped the citizens of Casper might be sympathetic enough to Ellie's cause to do something other than stand by and see her murdered. He had said as much to Ellie.

'How long do you think we can hold out for?' she asked between firing, crouching down behind one of the wagons.

'A while,' was Durbin's reply. 'We've got plenty of ammo. If help's coming, it'll be here soon.'

As he and Ellie talked, Bothwell and his men remounted their horses and began to charge.

'Are they mad?' Durbin asked himself when he saw what was happening. 'Aim at Bothwell,' he called out to this men. 'Everyone aim at Bothwell.'

They did so but, as if protected by some demonically impenetrable shield, Bothwell kept coming at them. As did at least half of his men and Ellie Watson's men began to suffer their first casualties. O'Brien was the first to be hit. Seeing that Bothwell and his men were practically on top of them, he had hurried to be at Ellie's side to shield her from their bullets, which were now being fired at close range.

'Get down,' he just had time to say to her, before a bullet hit him in the chest and he slumped, fatally wounded, against the wagon, his eyes full of regret, as if to apologize to Ellie for letting her down in this way.

As others of her men began to fall, Ellie felt a greater anger than ever at what Bothwell had done to her. She knew she was going to die but was determined he was going to die first. She had clung to the wagon for cover but now she stepped away from it and with a Colt .44 blasting from each hand she began to look for Bothwell. It was obvious to Bothwell's men who she was and for this reason none of them wanted to fire directly at her. The West's code of protectiveness of women was strong in them and they could not easily break it. But they fired all around her. Durbin took a hit in the left shoulder but was somehow able to keep firing. The young cowboy so far was lucky and was unhurt. But when he saw Ellie stepping out into the open he felt he had to rush to her side to help her.

'What you doing?' he called out to her, firing off rounds at the horsemen who were besieging them.

But Ellie did not answer him, for just as he reached her side she saw Bothwell. She would have killed him, had her guns not simultaneously run out of ammunition.

'Damn!' she exclaimed, pulling their triggers over and over again in disbelief.

She decided she'd have to reload them. As she turned to go back to the wagon, where there was a box of bullets, Bothwell spotted her. The young cowboy saw him do so and as Bothwell aimed his gun at her threw himself in front of her. Bothwell's shot went wide. The young cowboy fired one of his, which did not miss its mark. At less than a few yards range, it thumped into Bothwell's chest, knocking him flying from his horse.

Ellie, who had reached the box of bullets and was busily reloading her six guns, did not see him fall. Nor did she get the chance to rejoin the battle, for suddenly everything seemed to go quiet around her. As she looked up to see why, she became aware that Bothwell's men were riding away. Why? she asked herself. Then the answer became apparent. For there, towering above her mounted on their horses, was Sheriff Conner, Jerry Wheeler and the others, one of whom she thought she recognized as Tom Sun, another of the big-shot landowners in the county.

She turned to look for Durbin. Where was he? she asked herself, looking around desperately. Then she saw him, lying in a collapsed state at the bottom of the wagon.

'Henry!' she called, rushing up to him.

He heard but was barely able to reply.

'Thank God,' he said to her, as she leaned over him. 'Thank God you're all right.'

Ellie saw the wound in his shoulder but did not consider it to be fatal.

'Yeah, I survived,' Ellie said to him, 'and you're gonna be all right, too.'

Durbin couldn't believe her. He didn't want to.

'I got something I've got to tell you,' he said to her weakly.

'Not now,' Ellie said to him in comforting tones, looking around her at Sheriff Conner and the others.

'No . . .' Durbin began, but Ellie's attention was taken by Sheriff Conner asking her if she was all right.

Ellie did not answer Conner immediately, but instead looked around her. It seemed that only she and the young cowboy had

156

been left standing. And she supposed that Bothwell had got away.

'All right?' she at last answered Conner in a mocking tone of voice. 'What do you think?'

Before Conner could reply, that was if he had an answer to give, the young cowboy walked up to her, saying:

'I got him, miss, I got him. Bothwell's dead.'

Ellie looked at him in disbelief.

'Dead?' she asked, barely able to credit it.

'Yeah,' the young cowboy replied, smiling through his exhaustion. 'Dead.'

Ellie turned back to Durbin. 'Did you hear that, Henry? He's dead.'

But Durbin didn't hear anything. What Ellie hadn't seen was that he had taken a bullet in the back. Straight into his right kidney.

'Oh no,' Ellie said, suddenly finding herself overwhelmed by emotion and falling against Durbin. 'Oh no, Hal. Oh no.'

Bothwell was indeed dead, which enabled the Wyoming Stock Growers' Association to damn and disown him as one of their own. People who survived against the odds to come out on top were much admired by people in the West. Expedience played the biggest part in the admiration and respect that was subsequently shown to Ellie Watson by the Association. They'd realized that she was somebody they wanted to have on their side and when Bothwell's spread came up for its probate sale they made sure she got credit enough from the bank they controlled to afford it. It was an irony that was not lost on the people of Sweetwater County.

As for Durbin's secret, it went to the grave with him. The only other person who was privy to it was Sheriff Conner and he had his own reasons for keeping quiet about it. Even as he frequented Ellie Watson's rebuilt and hugely popular roadhouse, he kept his mouth shut.